SIGHT SEERING

SHADY GROVE PSYCHIC MYSTERY, BOOK 3

ADA BELL

A SEER IN THE CITY...

While visiting an estate sale to pick up new items for Missing Pieces, Aly gets hit with a surprise: the elderly homeowner didn't have a heart attack--she was murdered. Aly's got the evidence in her hands, and the killer is offering to sell it to her. Time to make a deal, then call the police.

If only anyone believed her. Miriam Peabody was in her 70s and appeared to die of natural causes. Police found no evidence of foul play, but Aly knows what she saw. Worse, she's pretty sure the killer has powers of their own. As she seeks evidence to support her vision, someone is watching Aly's every move. They're always one step ahead. She needs to find concrete evidence to give the police before someone Miriam trusted gets away with murder.

To Annette, Amy, and Kristen

In no way should my treatment of Aly's sister-in-law
be cause for concern

CHAPTER ONE

The rehab facility looked more like a golf course than a place to house people recovering from addiction. Sprawling emerald lawns framed a gorgeous two-story log house with massive windows. Even the name, Destiny's Haven, made me think of a retreat for psychics. Never would I have guessed that this was a dry-out center. Which was probably the point. Located across the border between Shady Grove and Willow Falls, the property sat a couple of hours from Lake Placid, a popular destination for tourists.

The parking lot was only about a third full when I pulled in, so I found a space easily and wiped my damp palms on the seats of my used Prius before getting out of the car.

Element one was hydrogen. Element two was helium. Element three was lithium.

Reciting the elements of the periodic table calmed me, and the thought of confronting my brother's former sister-in-law filled me with terror. Even knowing she couldn't do anything to me in a building full of nurses, counselors, and security didn't help much.

This was important, I reminded myself. I needed to do this for Kevin and Kyle. My three-year-old nephew deserved to know what happened to his mother, and Mary could be the key to finding that out.

Finally, my nerves settled enough to open the car door and walk inside. I moved quickly before my anxiety sent me scurrying back to the safety of the parking lot.

The dark-haired woman behind the desk greeted me with a huge smile befitting a concierge. Her name tag identified her as Harmony, a name that acted as a preview of the rich, gorgeous tone of her voice. "Welcome to Destiny's Haven! May I have your name, please?"

"Aly Reynolds," I said. "I'm here to see Mary Towne."

"I'm sorry." She looked up at me. "I don't have an Aly on the list, miss."

I resisted the urge to grind my teeth. "Does it say Aluminum?"

"Yes, it does."

"That's me. My brother thinks he's funny." I pulled out my wallet to show my driver's license, which unfortunately displayed the full version of my name. "It's a long story."

"You have my sympathies."

"Thanks."

"Tell me something," I said to Harmony as she led me down the hall to the family visitation room. "Are patients here allowed to come and go at will?"

According to Kevin, his wife's sister had been admitted to the local rehab facility shortly after Katrina died a little over a year ago. As far as we knew, she'd been living here ever since. I hadn't had any clue Mary lived near Shady Grove. But a couple of weeks ago, someone claiming to be her called, asking to meet and talk about some family stuff.

We met, she gave me a "gift" for Kyle that turned out to

be cursed, and then she vanished. When I went back to her house to confront her, a realtor told me no one lived there. He'd never heard of Mary. Imagine my surprise when Kevin then told me Mary was here, living in Destiny's Haven, where she'd been since Katrina died. I had about a billion questions, so here I was, looking for answers.

I didn't know if Mary had checked out of the facility briefly and pretended to live in that empty house or if I'd met someone else. Having only met Mary twice—at Kevin and Katrina's wedding, then her funeral—anyone with a passing resemblance probably could've fooled me. I'd only been fourteen at the wedding, and most of my time at both events had been spent with my family.

Hence my question to Harmony. If the woman staying here could have left to meet me, that information might help me figure out what happened.

Maybe.

"We prefer to call them 'guests' rather than patients," she said. "But yes, some people gain check-out privileges after a while. They can leave for short periods of time. This is a voluntary facility. We don't hold anyone against their will."

"Interesting, thanks. Do they have to say where they're going?"

"They don't, but if they come back drunk or high, they lose the privilege. They either are denied re-entry or are put on restrictions."

Hmm. Maybe Mary had...broken into a rental house to trick me into coming to see her? That still didn't make sense. Why not just call and invite me here? Or use her own home —Kevin had said she lived in the area before Katrina died. If she owned that house, she might still have it. I should check the property records.

We turned a corner, and Harmony led me through a set of French double doors. The room was light and airy, not at all what I'd expected. Under the welcoming scent of coffee, I detected disinfectant, as if the room was scrubbed regularly. About a dozen people watched television, played games, knitted, or worked on other various activities. Some sat in pairs chatting. One teenage boy painted an older man —from what I could tell, he'd created an excellent likeness.

A woman with long honey-colored hair sat at a table in the corner, playing chess by herself. Mary, right where Kevin said she would be. As I watched, she moved a piece, stood up, walked to the other side of the board, made another move, and returned. She even had a time clock.

Warily, I approached. Since I didn't know who I'd find here, I hadn't called in advance (other than to check the hours).

"Mary? You've got a visitor," Harmony said.

The woman looked up and gazed at me without a shred of recognition on her face. She had Katrina's heart-shaped lips and wide-brown eyes. Other than the total absence of warmth in her eyes and lack of makeup, she looked like the woman I'd met last week. A talented actress? Or someone else entirely?

"Hello," I said. "I'm Kevin's sister, Aly. Do you mind if I join you?"

"Do you know how to play chess?"

Not really, but well enough to let her beat me. "I do."

"Then please, have a seat." She gestured to the other side. "It's your turn."

I sat down to study the board, trying to recall how all the pieces moved. Harmony reminded us that lunch was in an hour, then headed back to the front desk. As soon as she passed through the doorway, Mary leaned forward.

"Listen, you've got to help me," she hissed.

"So now you remember me?" My words sounded a bit hostile, but I couldn't help it. This whole situation was twisted.

"What?"

"I—" The look of sheer panic on her face stopped me. "Never mind. What do you need?"

"You've got to get me out of here," she said. "I'm not Mary!"

Her words hit me like a punch in the chest. Not Mary?

When the woman posing as Mary had skipped town and Kevin told me that Katrina's sister lived in a rehab facility near Willow Falls, I'd had no reason not to believe him. Then Harmony said residents here could come and go, and it seemed like maybe I'd met the real Mary after all—albeit, someone who was hiding something big. But now, my world flipped upside down.

There were two people who looked like Mary. One of them claiming to be her and the other...stuck here against her will? Why didn't she leave? That was apparently allowed for anyone not on restrictions.

To avoid openly gaping, I picked up one of the chess pieces on the board and moved it...somewhere else. If that turned out to be a legit move, I'd buy a lottery ticket on the way home.

"Who are you, then? Are you the one I met a few weeks ago? The person who showed me family photos and gave me a rocking horse for Kyle? Because I have to say, she looked a lot like you."

The woman in the house had been more polished than the Mary sitting before me, but this woman was clean-faced, in yoga pants and her hair skimmed back. The other Mary wore professional clothes and makeup. I couldn't swear if they were the same person or not. Was she talking about body swappers?

"I know we look alike, but I'm not her. What rocking horse?"

The "family heirloom" I'd been given had a protective spell on it that attacked my boss and mentor, Olive. If this woman gave it to me, I had a few choice words to share before I gave her any assistance. Especially because the horse was meant for me or my nephew. I hadn't had my psychic powers long, but I didn't appreciate someone trying to zap them away.

A look of confusion crossed her face. Real or feigned? "No, listen to me—"

"You!" A girl who probably wasn't even my age came over and yanked on my elbow. "Get out of my seat!"

"Your seat?"

"Taylor. What are you doing?" Mary stood to address the newcomer. All of a sudden, I felt trapped in my tiny wooden chair, up against the wall with the two of them between me and the exit.

"My seat! I just went to the bathroom for a sec!"

"You haven't been in here all morning. I was playing a game with my friend here."

"Liar!" Taylor grabbed a fistful of Mary's hair and yanked. Mary shrieked, a sound of pain that turned to rage when Taylor showed her the handful of hair she'd removed and dropped it onto the chessboard. I watched, too stunned to intervene. "That's what happens to bad people who lie."

Harmony rushed up. "Taylor! Stop that right now. Get away from Mary!"

She spoke quickly into a walkie-talkie on her belt. Two burly men rushed into the room. A moment later, Taylor had been ushered out, and Mary sank to the floor, shaking.

I started to go to her. Harmony put one long arm out to stop me. "I'm sorry, but you need to leave."

"I didn't do anything, I swear. I was just sitting here when Taylor attacked me."

"That's true," Mary began, but Harmony wouldn't let her finish.

"Be that as it may, there's been a disturbance. Your presence triggered it, even if it was unintentional. Our residents come here for peace and quiet."

"I just need five minutes to talk to my sister-in-law."

(Sister-in-law-in-law? I still wasn't totally clear on what my relationship to Mary was.)

Most people hearing Mary's claims would conclude that she'd lost her mind, that the drugs or alcohol addled her brains so much she didn't know who or where she was. Most people weren't me. At the beginning of this year, I learned I was psychic. Since then, I'd met other psychics and witches and aura readers. A lookalike spell? Body-swapping? As far as I was concerned, anything was possible now.

Harmony placed herself between me and Mary. She knelt on the ground, glaring up at me. "If you're not out of here in thirty seconds, I'll have you removed."

Getting thrown out by security didn't appeal at all, but I needed to make one more effort. "If you're not Mary, who are you? How did you get here?"

Harmony sighed. "Oh, dear. Not that hogwash again. Come with me. We need to have another session." She helped Mary to her feet, then jabbed a finger in my direction. "You. Out. Now."

I wanted to argue with her, but then one of the men who'd taken Taylor returned. He headed straight for me. I didn't give him a chance to cross the room. Just yanked something off the table and bolted for a side exit, praying it wasn't locked.

An alarm sounded as the door open. Uh-oh. Shouts rang out behind me. I kicked into high speed, tearing across the grounds toward the safety of my car. It took probably a hundred yards before I realized no one was chasing me. They'd wanted me out, and now I was out. Unfortunately, I couldn't think of any way back in there without them calling security.

What a mess. Who was the woman inside? Harmony had instantly dismissed the claim she wasn't Mary as nonsense, as if she heard it all the time. Was either "Mary" I met Katrina's sister, or was there a third, real Mary out there somewhere?

With a groan of frustration, I kicked the rear tire of my car.

Then I remembered the item still clutched in my right hand. I'd only had one chance to grab something that would tell me if the woman sitting at the table was telling the truth. A couple of months ago, I'd learned that I could have visions by using objects that belonged to other people. My powers weren't completely developed yet, so I couldn't always see what I wanted, but that never stopped me from trying.

A piece from the chess set Mary played with might have helped me call up a vision of her past—but that wouldn't necessarily tell me who she was. I couldn't just touch something and see whatever I wanted to know, unfortunately. That would be too easy. When I used an object that belonged to someone else, I could often see important moments in the object's owner's life. Sometimes that was the day they died. Once I saw someone steal a Daytime Emmy Award. My gifts worked in mysterious—and sometimes hilarious—ways.

I could get images of literally any major event in the life of the person who owned the set or someone who used it regularly. The facility probably owned the set, and I'd guess at a minimum, several dozen people had used it over the years. Meaning that the chess pieces weren't likely to contain the information I needed.

But one thing in life had never let me down: science. Uncurling my fist, I looked at the item I'd pulled off the table on my way out the door: the chunk of hair Taylor yanked out of Mary's head.

"Not Mary, huh? We'll see about that."

CHAPTER TWO

After leaving Destiny's Haven, I put on my wireless headset and called Olive. This might have seemed like a weird time to call my boss, but she was so much more than that. She was my mentor, confidante, and future mother-in-law.

Er, scratch that last part. She didn't know about my dreams of marrying her son, probably because we weren't actually dating yet. But if I had any say in it, we would be soon. Sam was amazing: smart, kind, good-looking...and very distracting. While I was reliving the breath-taking kiss we'd shared a few weeks ago, Olive answered the phone, and I almost forgot why I'd called.

"Aly? Using the phone to call someone? Cough twice if you need me to call 911."

Yet another reason to love her. I'd gotten into some interesting situations since we met, but she was always willing to help.

"Sorry, Olive. I'm fine, just driving. I've got a question for you." Since she already knew about my search for Katrina's killer, it didn't take long to fill her in on the morning's events. "I realize how gross this sounds, but if I brought you the chunk of hair, could you tell me who it belonged to?"

"No."

Huh. I hadn't expected that response. "Just like that? You won't even try?"

Her voice softened. "Sorry, Aly. There are two reasons I can't. First, my powers don't work that way. I can't track humans. Loose hairs, lost eyelashes, dead skin cells... I don't know if it's because they're technically living beings rather than objects or because the fibers are too small, but I've never had any luck with them. When I was in college, I tried a few times, but nothing ever came of it."

"Darn it. So much for taking the easy route," I said. "You said there were two reasons you couldn't help. What's the other one?"

"You know who the hair came from. I'd only get a vision of that woman. That doesn't answer your question."

Good point. I didn't need an image of the woman who claimed not to be Mary. I needed to know who she actually was. "Ah, well. Thanks, anyway. Guess I'll have to go to the science lab."

"Are you going to do a DNA test?"

"I'm going to try." I chuckled. "Guess I should've signed up for genetics instead of molecular biology and chemistry. But at least I have lab access."

To be honest, I wasn't sure I had any idea how to do what I wanted, but after waiting so long to find Katrina's killer and finally getting a break, I had to try.

The hair I'd gotten from Mary (it was hard not to think of her that way, although I should really start calling her Subject A or something until I knew her identity) had strong roots. That was good—I knew from my high school science classes that you couldn't pull DNA from a loose hair on someone's sweater. There needed to be roots attached to extract a profile. Then, to find out who this woman was, I needed to compare her information to a known entity.

Since the real Mary was my sister-in-law's older sister, that should have been easy. They indisputably had the same mother, and therefore the same mitochondrial DNA. Mitochondrial DNA was the best way to figure this stuff out. Unfortunately, Katrina was dead. After my sister-in-law died, my brother moved all of her belongings to a storage facility in the small town where they'd lived. While searching the basement, I'd found the key, but it was two-and-a-half hours away. Even if he'd kept an old hairbrush or toothbrush—and why would he? Ew—I couldn't get to the storage facility easily. Between school and work, there hadn't been any way to get there without arousing Kevin's suspicion. No access to Katrina's DNA yet.

I did, however, have the next best thing: her son, Kyle. Half of his DNA would belong to my brother, but I should be able to extract that from the sample and compare what remained. Hopefully. With luck and maybe the kindness of a bored lab assistant. Most of my college friends were also studying biology. I wasn't sure if any of them would have the knowledge to help without taking over and possibly ruining everything. (Okay, only one of my friends was likely to do that, but I definitely couldn't ask her for help on this experiment.)

Turned out, I couldn't drive straight to the lab, anyway. Despite the chaos of wrappers, Goldfish crackers, half-empty cups, and random garbage in Kyle's car seat, there was no DNA sample. I didn't love the idea of trying to extract his DNA from a quarter-inch of crusty milk that smelled so terrible, I paused to throw the cup in the garbage before driving home. Cups were cheap, and I couldn't distill DNA while trying not to puke. Saliva only carried little bits of genetic material, anyway.

My brother wasn't likely to let me take a cheek swab, and Kyle was old enough that he'd probably mention it without thinking. Hmm. Maybe I could tell my brother we were doing paternity tests for one of my courses? He probably didn't know I wouldn't be taking genetics until next year.

I shook my head. Nah, the easiest way would be to snatch Kyle's toothbrush or hairbrush after he went to bed for the night. I could hide it in my backpack and take it to the lab.

When I got home and my brother asked how my visit to Destiny's Haven went, I simply told him we were attacked by another resident and Mary seemed upset. All true. If he suspected I was hiding something, he didn't mention it. Then I dove into my research so I'd have a plan before I got to the lab.

After Kyle went to bed for the night, I swiped his toothbrush and stuck it in my backpack. At the last minute, I decided to clean out Kevin's hairbrush, too, just in case. If the samples were similar, I wanted the ability to exclude Kevin's genetic material from the comparison. Assuming I could figure out how to do that.

To my great relief, when I made it to the lab, only three other students sat inside. The first was a girl I didn't recognize, pouring some smoking liquid into multiple flasks. Not an experiment I wanted to interrupt. At the table behind her sat Brad Stephens from my Molecular Biology class, which surprised me a bit. When we'd met, he'd been very much a "no one cares about learning" member of the basketball team. The Brad I'd first met wouldn't have been caught dead in the school science lab outside of a scheduled class. He claimed to have gone through an epiphany recently, so the sight of him hunched over a microscope made me smile.

We nodded at each other, but I didn't go talk to him. Too much to do. The Lab Assistant overseeing the open lab time sat at a bench in the front, reading a romance novel. He hid it under a copy of *National Geographic* when I approached.

"I'm Porter," he said. "Can I help you?"

After showing my student ID, I said, "I was wondering if we have a PRC machine here?"

The technique used to distill DNA from a sample was called Polymerase Chain Reaction. According to my online research, most college-level science labs would have one. It turned out I was in luck: we had two.

Porter led me to them, pointing out other items the internet assured me would be needed. "We've got chloroform and distilled water in that cupboard, along with the other supplies. Do not use the tap water, please. It gunks everything up, and I'll get yelled at for not telling you."

"No problem. Thanks for the reminder."

He continued, "The gel you'll need to see the DNA is on this shelf. It's the ethidium bromide."

That book must've been pretty good, because he didn't ask what I was doing or if I needed any help. I thanked him, and he went back to the bench. A moment later, the book was nowhere to be seen, but Porter seemed very interested in something in his lap.

Before getting started, I recited the elements of the periodic table to calm my nerves and still my shaking hands. Bromine was element thirty-five, chemical symbol BR. Same color as iodine. A cooler first name than "Aluminum." Also a key ingredient of this experiment.

Distilling DNA was a tricky business, especially considering my fear that I'd mess it up and never get another sample from "Mary." I couldn't exactly waltz back into Destiny's Haven after what happened. Or, you know, rip out another chunk of her hair. I started with Kyle's toothbrush, since I could get more DNA from that any time I convinced him to brush his teeth. Once or twice a month, surely.

To start, the machine manipulated the temperatures to replicate the DNA. This took some time. Eventually, I got it going—only needing to enlist Porter's assistance twice. Luckily, he didn't ask what I was doing. Then I sat down to work on other homework while the machines did their things. After a couple of hours, I had results! Not final results, just something to work with: two mitochondrial DNA samples. One from Kyle. One from the woman formerly-(currently?)-known as Mary.

The human body contains loads of genes, but luckily, I didn't have to compare them all. That would take forever, and much of the information would be useless for my purposes. I isolated four standard DNA markers for comparison, then put one slide each on two adjacent microscopes.

If the woman I met was Kyle's aunt, the samples would match, although with possibly some slight mutations. They shared a grandmother, not a mother, so the genetic material might not be exactly the same. Hopefully, I'd be able to tell the difference between a mutation and two non-matching samples.

For five minutes, I went back and forth, blinking, rubbing my eyes, and comparing the two slides. Then I isolated four more genetic markers and ran the tests again. And again. This needed to be right.

After about an hour of this, Porter came over. "You know, checking repeatedly doesn't give you the results you want."

"To be honest, I'm not sure what results I was hoping for," I said.

"Baby daddy?" He nodded. "Happens a lot."

It wasn't worth trying to explain. "Uh, yeah."

I turned back to the slides for what felt like the thousandth time. It turned out minor gene mutations weren't an issue.

From what I could tell, the genetic markers on the samples were a match. Mary and Kyle shared a female relative.

Why had Mary lied to me? What game was she playing?

CHAPTER THREE

The day after my disastrous visit, Kevin had called Destiny's Haven and asked about Mary. He used his fancy lawyer voice. They told him she was not accepting visitors or phone calls until further notice, leaving me desperate to figure out how to talk to her. I assumed they wouldn't give her mail from me, but I sent a letter, anyway. If she didn't answer, my best plan involved dressing as a janitor and sneaking in late at night. That seemed like a great way to wind up in prison.

The following Saturday, I wasn't any closer to finding a way to get back in to see Mary (or whoever she was). Calls to Destiny's Haven were politely rejected no matter what time of day or night I tried. The people who answered the phone now recognized my voice, and some of them hung up before I even got out a full sentence. It wasn't worth driving out there and asking them to let me see her. Not after the way I'd been chased out for being attacked by another resident.

Instead, I had another project to focus on: visiting an estate sale as a representative of Missing Pieces. The executor, Barry Rosenberg, had called Olive and invited her to attend under the pretext of picking up a few items for sale in the store. However, she'd told me privately that Barry was the father of an old friend, and he'd asked for help investigating who owned some potentially stolen items.

For many years, rumors had circulated that Barry's late client, Liam Peabody, made his money not in the stock market but as a thief. Now that Liam's wife had also passed away, as executor, Barry wanted to verify the paintings he'd found. Everyone knew the Peabody house had some gorgeous pieces, but where had they come from? Did art thieves display their booty in their homes? I didn't know, and apparently, Barry didn't, either. Before involving police in old rumors and bringing negative attention to his clients, he wanted Olive to read the works of art.

She asked me to come watch her work, an opportunity I jumped at. Ever since I'd had my first vision in her store, Olive had been helping me develop my powers. Watching her work could only help, plus I'd get a chance to learn the business side of the antique store.

Olive didn't actually need me for any of this. She probably invited me because the estate was near New York City, where Sam lived. She knew I had an enormous crush on Sam (although she didn't know about our kiss). We hadn't managed a date because of the hundred miles of highway between our homes, but if I were already in a suburb, we could probably manage dinner.

She'd barely finished asking me if I was willing to go to the sale before I accepted. I even packed an overnight bag in case I could find a way to fake a flat tire and ensure that Sam and I wound up sharing the last empty bed at a deserted motel. Porter at the science lab wasn't the only one who read romance novels.

Shortly after lunchtime, Olive turned into a driveway at the bottom of a long, sloping hill. The house rose high on the horizon, towering above the scenery. A wrought-iron gate around the outside informed anyone who couldn't tell from the hedge maze and the massive grounds that whoever lived here had serious money.

As directed, we parked around the back. Barry met us at a door that looked suspiciously like a servant's entrance. For some reason, the idea of an older estate lawyer made me think of someone staid, boring. Barry answered the door wearing a mustard-colored plaid jacket and a wide smile. His hair reminded me of Doc Brown in those old movies about time travel, and he exuded the vibe of someone who loves life.

"Thank you so much for coming," Barry said. "I wanted to get this taken care of sooner, but there were some issues getting access to all the pieces."

"Of course! I'm excited. Aly and I are going to the city after we leave here. Then I'm off to see *Hamilton* with my wife while Aly has a date." Olive shot me a knowing look, which I pointedly ignored. We might be more friends than employee/employer, but I wasn't ready to share the details of my budding relationship with the guy's mom.

"I've never been," I added. "Olive promised to show me around Times Square."

"You'll love it," Barry said. "I'm glad I could give you a reason to come down. Let's head inside."

Images, scents, and sounds assailed me from the moment I crossed the threshold. The smell of cinnamon and sugar in the air, the clatter of dishes and conversation, a broken plate shattering, a clock ticking. Some of the sensations may be real, but most were fully inside my head. With a gasp, I leaned against the kitchen doorway. Olive gave me the job at Missing Pieces because of my psychic abilities, but never had I been in a place with so many objects seeking to tell me something at once.

Normally, I had to pick up and use an object to learn anything, but—this house had a story it wanted to share. I made a mental note to ask Olive whether she'd ever experienced anything similar as soon as Barry left us alone.

"Are you okay?" Barry asked.

"Yes, sorry. I tripped."

Behind Barry's back, Olive shot me a look suggesting she didn't believe me, but she didn't comment.

When we entered the living room, my mouth dropped open. Working in an antique store, I was used to being surrounded by fabulous stuff most of the time. But many of Mrs. Peabody's belongings were high, high quality. The kind of thing that didn't last long on the shelves but paid the rent when it showed up. Also the kind of thing that would look incredible in my new apartment if I ever moved out of my brother's house. Not that I could afford any of it.

Several buffets along the back wall displayed a gorgeous collection of pink and white china. I didn't even want to think about what it cost. Did estate sales allow installment plans? Tables placed end to end around the room boasted silverware, candlesticks, picture frames, placemats, coffee pots—everything you'd ever think to put in your kitchen and a million things you wouldn't. There were things I couldn't even identify.

Of course, I didn't cook. People who did would probably recognize this kitchen mélange.

All of a sudden, the buzz of the house fell away. My hearing returned to normal, like when the airplane landed and your ears popped. So weird.

"Are you okay?" Olive asked.

"I think so." I shook my head to clear it and kept my voice low. "There was a strange energy in this place when we walked in. Not sure how else to describe it, but it's gone now."

Barry turned around. "Is something wrong?"

"No, everything is great!" I lied. "Miriam had so many beautiful pieces, I wish I could buy them all."

"She did have excellent taste." A faraway look came over him, as if recalling a specific memory. The sadness in his eyes reminded me that we weren't here to work and shop. A woman had died, and she had friends and family who cared about her. We needed to be mindful of their feelings while we went through her husband's belongings (and potentially labeled him a thief).

Before I could think what to say, Olive leaned forward and put one hand on his arm. "It's okay."

"Thank you. Let's go upstairs."

As we neared the front hallway, a tornado of a woman burst into the living room. Short, black hair framed her pale face. Heavy makeup ringed her brown eyes, giving her the longest and thickest eyelashes I'd ever seen. A similar-looking man trailed in her wake, moving as if the two of them formed a human negative correlation graph.

She zeroed in on us immediately. "Barry! I'm so sorry I'm unforgivably late. Traffic was abominable, as usual. Why does anyone drive in the city? Such a waste of time. I only keep my license to drive Aunt Miriam around." Her face fell. "Kept, I mean. I guess I can let it expire now. What a silly thing to be sad about."

Barry put one hand on her arm. "This is a difficult time for everyone. Olive, Aly, this is Deborah, Miriam's niece. Deborah, this is Olive and Aly from Missing Pieces.

They're going to take some items to their store after the sale."

"Missing Pieces? Hold on." She was quiet for a moment, and we let her think. "Are you the art experts? I told Barry that these paintings are legitimate. This whole idea of Uncle Liam as some kind of criminal mastermind is ridiculous. My uncle was as honest as the day is long."

Barry snorted quietly behind her, which he turned into a cough when all three of us turned to look at him.

"Well, we're happy to verify that your uncle purchased everything legitimately," Olive said.

Deborah ignored her and turned to Barry. "Really, this nonsense has gone on long enough. Next you'll help my dear brother look for booty buried under loose floorboards in the attic."

He turned red. "I'm just trying to do my job."

"Steal my money is more like it," she said. "Don't think I don't know you charge me by the hour for this. Excuse me. I need to get ready for the sale to make sure no one else is trying to bleed me dry."

"What an interesting lady," Olive commented as we again moved toward the staircase.

"Bleed her dry?" I asked tentatively.

"Miriam's only child died in Iraq," Barry said. "Deborah is her niece and sole heir. The estate pays me, not the heirs, but in her mind, it's all the same."

"That's tragic. I'm so sorry," Olive said.

I echoed her.

"Thank you." He swallowed and shook his head. "I guess I should give you some background. The Peabody family made a fortune in the hotel industry, starting around the turn of the nineteenth century. But Liam Peabody was a big fan of gambling, and rumor has it that he wasn't nearly as successful at it as his other pursuits."

"You think he gambled away the family fortune?"

"I don't know," he said. "Obviously, I can't tell you anything he confided in me."

"Of course not," Olive said. "We wouldn't expect you to."

I had a different answer all ready, but living with a lawyer had taught me all about confidentiality and privilege. If we wanted to know how much was in Liam's estate, we'd have to check the public probate court records.

Barry continued, "Liam lived as if he had all the money in the world. Anyone could see that. The two things he loved the most were good wine and expensive art, especially paintings."

We reached the top of the stairs and entered what must've once been a bedroom. At the moment, massive paintings sat up against every wall and on all of the furniture. I counted at least a dozen before I stopped.

"Where should we start?" Olive asked.

"If you don't mind, I've got a list here," Barry said. "Everything is numbered."

He directed her to a landscape. Considering my lack of art knowledge, that was about all I could tell anyone about it. The artist used green and blue and pink. It was pretty, although not my style.

Olive stepped forward, placed one hand on the painting, and closed her eyes. They popped open almost instantly.

CHAPTER FOUR

Barry and I stood breathlessly while Olive read the painting. He needed to know whether his former client was a thief. I just loved to watch her work. She took on this air of serenity, as if nothing in the world suited her as perfectly as reading an object and finding out who owned it.

"Well, this one's easy," she said. "It belongs to that rather hostile woman downstairs."

"To Deborah?" I said with surprise.

"As Miriam's heir, technically everything in this house belongs to her," Barry said. "I assume that's why she's showing up."

Olive nodded. "Probably. She is the one in my vision. Now this next piece...I'm seeing a couple, probably in their late fifties. They look a little older than me. Middle Eastern descent, I'd say. I don't know who they are, but neither of them looks like Deborah."

"Here is Liam and Miriam's most recent photo, taken a few years before he died." Barry handed Olive a picture of a well-dressed elderly white couple. "Is that them?"

Immediately, she said, "No. The painting is borrowed or stolen. I don't know which, but they're not the owners."

Barry made a note. "If I show you some pictures, do you think you could identify the owners from your vision?"

"Certainly. Aly, this could take a while. Why don't you poke around downstairs?"

"Sure. Want me to take this painting?" I gestured at the one that belonged to Deborah, since it would presumably be for sale now.

"Oh, no," Barry said. "If you dropped it, you'd owe the estate about four thousand dollars."

I gulped and headed for the door, hands high to avoid touching anything by mistake.

Downstairs, I spotted Deborah behind a table, surveying the room. Although the estate sale started at nine, there weren't a lot of people here. Maybe most people came and left early. Or maybe they were wandering around outside, looking at those amazing gardens.

She didn't look happy to see me, but maybe some good news would help. "You'll be happy to know the first painting Olive looked at was legitimate."

"Of course it was." She gave me a tight smile. "Sorry about before. You wouldn't believe the things that have happened since Aunt Miriam died. People talking about art thieves and buried treasure and—what a nightmare."

"I can't even imagine what you're going through," I said honestly. "It must be tough."

"Thanks. Anyway, I know you're here to work, but feel free to take a look around. Let me know if you see anything you want to buy."

"So far, I want to buy it all," I said with a laugh. "Unfortunately, I don't have a lot of space. I live in my brother's spare bedroom."

"I understand. I have a four-hundred square foot studio apartment in the city."

That was shockingly close to the size of my room at Kevin's. New York City real estate baffled me. Since I had nothing to say about tiny homes, instead, I asked, "Were you and Miriam close?"

"She was my favorite aunt," she said with a slight sniffle. "Sorry, it's been a rough couple of weeks. We all thought Aunt Mir was going to outlive us. She and I made plans to travel the world together, you know. I bought us cruise tickets just a couple of weeks ago. The ship sails next month. I can't quite believe she's gone."

Her speech seemed wooden, a bit practiced. Then again, she'd probably said it forty times in the past few weeks.

"It must've been quite a shock to lose her so suddenly," I said.

"Thank you, yes. Even though she was in her seventies, I never thought of her as old or frail. I thought we had so much time left. At least she's at peace now." She stopped and looked around. "Listen to me go on. I'm going to scare away all the buyers with my ramblings."

"She really did have a beautiful home," I said. "So many nice things."

"I always loved this house." She studied me for a moment. "What made you decide to work in antiques? Seems odd for someone so young."

Me? Well, antiques provide a conduit for my psychic powers, I didn't say. Instead, I opted for a partial truth. "My grandmother was a collector. I like being around things that remind me of her."

"That's sweet." Deborah gestured to the items on the

table behind us. "Are you doing any shopping for yourself while you're here?"

I shifted my gaze to the objects for sale. When I'd first walked in, they'd hummed at me. Maybe it was the sheer number of items belonging to a single person, but I'd never gotten such strong readings solely from being near stuff. If I wasn't careful, I'd experience every single moment of Miriam's life before I left, all in micro-second flashes on fast-forward. From what Barry had told Olive, that would include some pretty boring visions. Married at eighteen, lived to seventy-four, very wealthy, died in her sleep of natural causes.

Well, that was what I'd thought earlier. After our conversation with Barry, I added an item to my mental list: possibly married to an art thief. Suddenly, Miriam looked a little more interesting.

"Both, I suppose. I've been looking for a formal tea service for a couple of months now. I love the idea of having my friends over and serving them on a china tray." I avoided her gaze. "Yes, it's silly."

"Not all. Let me see what we have."

She wandered off to the right, and I moved toward the nearest china cabinet. Immediately, I spotted a stunning off-white teapot that Deborah had bypassed. A large pink and blue bouquet was painted on the side, with pink accents on the top. Gold handle and spout, with a golden tip on the lid. Real or paint, I didn't know. The same design adorned an adorable teeny milk pitcher. Half a dozen matching cups sat on the gold and pink tray. It quite literally took my breath away. Not just because of the design.

The teapot called to me. I heard it. My bones felt its siren's call.

Over the past few months, I'd learned a few tricks for

trying to induce a vision, and I practiced regularly. Some worked, many didn't. There were also ways to "cleanse" items, like my used car, to help avoid getting some poorly timed distractions. But this was different. Beyond a shadow of a doubt, I knew that if I picked up that tea set, I was going to have a vision.

A vision that, most likely, I wouldn't want anyone else to witness. Especially if there was a chance I'd drop this gorgeous, probably expensive antique. The fact that Deborah didn't offer to sell it to me suggested she didn't think I could afford it.

She stopped and saw me staring. "Do you like that one? The pattern seems a little fussy for someone your age."

I pretended I needed time to think about it. "Hmm. I'm not sure. Do you want to help someone else while I look around a little more?"

While we were talking, several more people had trickled through the doors. Now they filled the rooms, looking, touching, and asking questions. Surely, Deborah could talk to one of them while I had a quick conversation with the teapot.

Now that was a weird thought.

Someone jostled me out of the way. "How much is this?"

Out of habit, I moved away from the woman's sharp elbows before pausing to look at her. She looked about Deborah's age, which probably put her in her mid-forties. Guessing ages was not my strong suit. She had short, curly blonde hair, and her perfume made me gag with its pungency. I didn't know anyone under seventy wore perfume anymore. Whatever it was might have smelled okay if this woman hadn't bathed in it.

My first instinct was to bolt, but then I saw the item she pointed at, and my heart leapt into my throat.

"I'm sorry, but that's my tea set," I said.

The woman glared at me. "It's sitting on the shelf. It still has a sticker on it."

"I was just about to buy it," I said. "Deborah can tell you—"

"Debbie? Did this *girl* already purchase my tea set?"

Oh, no. I was about to say something—okay, I didn't actually know what—when Deborah pulled herself up to her full height and glared down her nose at the woman. "It's Deb-or-ah, Lindsay. We were just chatting about some of Aunt Miriam's belongings."

"That's nice. I'll pay you double whatever she offered. My mom would love this, and I want her to have it."

My stomach dropped. I hadn't offered anything yet because I probably couldn't afford the set. But I still needed it. While many of the objects had spoken to me over the past few months, none created the magnetic pull of this one. I didn't know if something particularly important had happened to Miriam while she used it or if the item sensed I'd been wanting to buy something similar—was that a thing? Either way, Lindsay couldn't have it.

"I don't think Miriam wanted your mom to have any of her things." Turning away from Lindsay's gasp, Deborah looked at me apologetically. "We'd talked about fifty dollars. Is that okay?"

The woman was a saint. We'd discussed no such thing. At Missing Pieces, it would cost about two-fifty, but I didn't know how estate sale prices compared.

"I'll give you a hundred," Lindsay said. "Wrap it up, Debbie."

"This isn't an auction." Deborah carefully but swiftly

stacked the cups and other pieces on the china tray, as if she wanted to keep her body between the set and Lindsay. "Aly, I believe we had a deal?"

"Yes, ma'am. Thank you so much." Before Lindsay could react, I reached out and snatched the teapot off the tray. It seemed like it needed me to protect it from her, although I realize how that sounded.

The second my fingers closed around the handle, a familiar sensation took hold, the feeling that told me a vision was imminent. Lindsay reached for it at the same time. The world started to tilt out from under me. Before I could so much as sit down to prepare myself for what was about to happen, the room vanished.

I sat in a high-backed chair with a floral pattern. Lines wrote a road map on the hands folded neatly in my lap. Green brocade wallpaper told me I sat in the same room now laid out for the estate sale. In the kitchen, my niece moved around, preparing tea.

After the move, I'd miss this old home, the cream-colored carpets, the high ceilings. But it was for the best. Time to move on. The house was drafty, it was lonely, and it was getting harder to move from one floor to the next.

Someone entered the room carrying a tray, which she set on the small wooden table beside the chair. Mrs. Peabody had terrible eyesight, because I had no idea who this person must be until I heard her voice. "Cream and one sugar, right?"

"Right." I nodded, pleased that she remembered. Deborah was such a good girl, always taking care of me. "Are you sure you don't mind helping me pack up everything? I can hire movers."

"Don't be silly," she said. "I'm not going to let strangers

toss all your stuff into boxes. They'll break your treasures. We'll do this together."

"You're a sweet girl."

"After all you've done for me, it's the least I can do."

Her words warmed my insides in the same way the tea would. I cradled the cup for a moment, savoring the slight, nutty odor. Then I took a sip.

Something was wrong. I held the tea in my mouth, tilting my head and letting it wash over my taste buds. With a wince, I swallowed.

"You must have burned the tea, dear," I said. "It's bitter."

All of a sudden, I couldn't breathe.

The cup fell to my lap. My hands clawed at my throat.

The world went black.

As a coughing fit racked my body, the room came back into focus. The same green wallpaper, the pattern much sharper in real-time than in my vision. Old floral carpet, clean but well-trod. The same woman who'd handed her aunt a poisoned cup of tea.

Poor Mrs. Peabody hadn't died peacefully in her sleep. She'd been murdered. By the woman standing in front of me.

When my world righted itself, Deborah was staring at me open-mouthed. Darn it. I knew better than to touch the teapot in front of her. Truly, though, I couldn't help myself. If that other woman had bought my set, I'd never have forgiven myself. She'd needed to be stopped.

With that reminder, I glanced around, but Lindsay was nowhere to be seen. Poor woman, I'd probably scared the willies out of her. I'd never seen myself have a vision, obviously, but the reactions I'd gotten from others told me they'd noticed. I'd have to track her down to apologize. Maybe I could pretend to get seizures or something.

Meanwhile, Deborah still watched me from across the table. The smile on her face was pasted on, the mask of perfect professionalism. Although she'd been flustered when she arrived, she was now flawless. Only the slightest twitching of her eyes betrayed that anything was wrong. She must've worked retail before inheriting a twenty-million-dollar estate.

"Is everything okay?"

"Yes, wonderful!" The words stuck in my throat. I

needed to get away from her. "This is, well, it's exactly what I've been looking for. I'd like to buy it, if that's okay."

"Well, yeah, that's why it's here. Everything must go."

"Right." My eyes went to the price tag, and I gulped. "You said it was fifty dollars before, right?"

"It's actually two hundred. I just didn't want Lindsay to get her grubby hands on it. I can't stand her."

"Is the price negotiable?"

"Considering that I shooed another buyer away, no." Deborah's eyes drilled holes into my face. If I didn't know better, I'd swear she'd seen inside my vision. "All prices final, I'm afraid. But like I said, you can wait and see if no one else wants it. Your boss might give you a discount after we donate it to the store. Assuming Lindsay doesn't return."

"Don't be ridiculous, darling." When I tried to act casual, sometimes I sounded like a sixty-year-old British woman. "My wallet is upstairs with Olive, though. Let me go find her. Back in a jiff."

I turned to go, still clutching the teapot to my chest.

"Sorry, but you're not allowed to walk around the house with unpurchased items," Deborah said. "I'd be happy to pack up the whole set and leave it in a box by the register. You can pick it up after you talk to your boss. That way, you're not juggling a bunch of china all afternoon."

Nope. The way she was looking at me one hundred percent made me not want to hand over the teapot. Even though she couldn't possibly know what I saw. Couldn't have any idea that I'd seen her kill her aunt. I pulled out my phone to text Olive, but there was no signal. Darn it. I could probably get enough to text, but who knew how long it would take her to check?

No big. Either she or Barry should pass through eventually. Meanwhile, maybe I could get some useful information. The vision told me Deborah killed her aunt, but not why. This could be my chance to get her talking.

"I'll just wait for her to finish examining the paintings," I said. "Tell me about your aunt. You must miss her a lot."

"Oh, yes, very much. I adored Aunt Miriam," she said. "She was the sweetest woman, always looking out for others. Everyone loved her. For the past couple of years, I've been here almost every week for one thing or another. Making sure contractors don't take advantage of her, playing tennis, stuff like that."

"Your job doesn't mind you taking so much time off?"

"My hours are pretty flexible. We're open nights and weekends, so they're good about letting me work on the weekend or a late shift when Aunt Miriam needs me. Needed me." She swallowed. "Sorry."

My eyes never left her face as she spoke, searching for any sign of a lie. She seemed genuinely upset. Tears shimmered in her eyes, and I wondered if she was a great actress or felt sorry for what she'd done.

"Tell me, are you going to be in Lunar Heights long?" she asked.

As long as it takes to prove you're a killer.

Instead, I said, "Just for today. I've never been to the city. Olive has tickets to *Hamilton* tonight, so I'm going to meet a friend, and we'll head back north later." The reminder of getting to see Sam brought a smile to my face.

"A 'friend' or a date?" She'd apparently picked up on my excitement. "You could climb the Empire State Building together! That's so romantic. I always wanted to go up there with a lover. The two of you could kiss, just like in *Sleepless in Seattle.*"

The thought brought a flush to my face. "Oh, we're not... I mean, uh..."

"Oh, sorry. Now I've stepped in it. From the look on your face, I thought he was your boyfriend. Does he know how you feel about him?"

Never did I ever think I'd be getting romantic advice from a murderer. "For now, we're just good friends. Mostly. Anywhere less romantic we could go?"

"My museum is hosting an exhibit tonight. Abaci Through the Ages. Math is pretty unromantic."

"You don't know Sam. He *loves* math stuff. So do I, to be honest."

"Perfect! Then you have to come. I'll add you and a guest to the list."

I had no intention whatsoever of actually going to hang out with her that evening, but I said thanks to avoid raising her suspicions. There was still no sign of Olive, so I needed to keep her talking. "Hold on. You work in a museum? Don't you want this stuff for yourself? Now I feel bad that Missing Pieces is going to swoop up all your treasures."

"Don't be silly," she said. "I'm happy to donate most of this. LaMonica is a math museum, mostly tech stuff. No paintings or sculptures like what you saw upstairs. Aunt Miriam hated the museum. Thought it was tacky because technology isn't 'real art' like her precious paintings. Not even these amazingly centuries-old abaci I managed to borrow for tonight's exhibit. It was the only thing we ever argued about."

Hmm. As motives went, killing someone for not liking your job seemed pretty weak. The fact that Deborah was Miriam's sole heir helped, of course, but they were friends. I didn't see a person disinheriting a relative because of a disagreement about what constituted art. It sounded like Deborah had a good job. Did she have some kind of problem where she needed money now? Couldn't she have asked for it?

Then again, what did I know? It wasn't like I had rich relatives desperate to give me cash.

"Sorry, I have to help some other people. Are you ready to buy the tea set?" Deborah asked.

"Right. I'm sorry. I'll go find Olive."

Looking desperately around the room, I saw no one. Finally, I realized that refusing to leave the teapot with the rest of the set would make Deborah suspicious and do nothing to bring Olive into the room faster. I held it out, but insisted I'd be right back. "Please hold this for me. Five minutes. I'll be back before you know I'm gone."

"Uh-huh." She wasn't even listening anymore, eyes zooming around the room as she looked for a buyer with actual cash.

I hated to leave the murder weapon with the killer but didn't have a choice. At least Lindsay was nowhere to be seen. I just needed to get the money and make it back to the house before she realized I'd left without my prize. Besides, Deborah didn't have any idea I knew what she'd done. I kept reminding myself of that.

Olive was still in the bedroom, exactly where I left her. Someone had been moving the paintings around, apparently, because they were now in three stacks against the far wall. I couldn't help noticing that the one she'd identified as belonging to the estate stood alone.

The color drained from her face when she saw me. I didn't want to think about how I must look. "Barry, would you mind getting me a glass of water? I'd like to talk to Aly for a moment."

"Of course. I should have offered you something earlier. My apologies."

"I'm glad you're here," Olive said when the door shut behind Barry. "I want you to try an experiment."

My ears perked up. My inner scientist *loved* experiments. "Okay, but before I do, you should know that I just had a psychic vision of Miriam drinking poisoned tea and I can't buy the item that gave it to me unless you loan me one hundred ninety dollars."

Olive blinked several times. "I'll grab my checkbook. Keep talking."

With a glance at the door, I lowered my voice. "Mrs. Peabody didn't die in her sleep. She was planning to sell the house, so Deborah killed her."

"Start at the beginning."

As quickly as I could, I explained my vision. She dug around in her purse while I talked, finally coming up with a pen and checkbook. She immediately started writing.

"You don't seem surprised," I said when I got to the end of my vision.

"Not really," she said. "I invited you here because I suspected there was more to the story than Barry was telling me. It wouldn't be the first time someone killed a relative to get their inheritance early."

In the short time since I'd discovered my powers, I'd learned that people killed for more minor reasons than wanting to own a mansion.

As she handed me the check, Olive said, "Aly, you've got to tell someone what you saw."

"I will, as soon as I secure the evidence," I said. "First things first, I need to make sure no one else buys that tea set."

"Police will make sure of that when they arrive, you know. They'll confiscate it."

Hmm. I hadn't thought of that. Did I want to pay two

hundred dollars to buy an item that might be seized by police and held as evidence? No, but I was pretty sure the law said they'd have to give it back to me after trial. Or maybe Barry would give me a refund. Better to secure it now before someone else bought it. Another thought struck me.

"Why would police be here? They won't drop everything to rush over and investigate the death of a seventy-year-old woman based on the word of a psychic even in a rich place like Lunar Heights, will they?"

"Good point. Let's go get it."

Deborah smiled brightly when I returned with the check. Of course she did. My money (well, Olive's money, but I would pay her back) now belonged to her, because she killed for it. "Are you ready?"

"Absolutely." I held out my hands, hoping my loathing didn't show on my face. I'd never been much of an actress. "One antique pink and blue tea set, please."

"Sure thing." She dug around beneath the table. After a moment, she stood, one hand on her hip, the other against her face. Her eyes scanned stuff that I couldn't see.

"Is everything okay?"

"I know it was here somewhere," Deborah said.

"Let me look," I said impatiently.

I knew leaving the teapot with Deborah had been a bad idea. Knowing she'd killed her aunt wasn't going to be enough. That teapot had given me a vision, and it might be able to tell me more. If nothing else, I wanted to have it in hand when I went to tell the police what I'd seen. They could test the cups and the teapot for poison.

This wasn't Shady Grove. No one on the police force knew me, and I hadn't helped them solve crimes before. There was no reason to think anyone in Lunar Heights believed in psychics or would be willing to listen to me. Holding the teapot when I told them would give me strength. If there was actual poisonous residue on the china, that would give me credibility.

Deborah stepped aside, allowing me to look behind the table with her. It was just a card table covered by a plain white cloth. There were a few items back there, each with a tag and a name. I spotted an old end table, a candelabra, some lovely jewelry. But not my tea set. No box full of china, as promised. No cute little milk pitcher, not a single cup, no pot, not even the tray. All nine pieces, disappeared.

The blood drained from my face. Suddenly, I felt light-headed. I stumbled back around to the front of the table. Olive caught me as I fell.

"It's gone."

CHAPTER SIX

Deborah's words hung in the air like a little cartoon balloon attached to her mouth. I stared at her, completely dumbfounded. "What do you mean, gone?"

This couldn't be a coincidence. I saw her murder her aunt when I touched the tea set, stupidly left it in her care while I went to get enough money to pay for it, and now it was gone? No way did I buy that. She must have hidden it, although I couldn't think how she'd know to do that.

Only Olive's hand on my shoulder restrained me from throwing myself behind the row of tables to shake it out of Deborah. Her voice sounded much more pleasant than I felt. "Can you look again, please?"

"Sure." Deborah ran one hand through her hair and bent down, still rummaging. After a moment, just when I was about to scream with frustration, she straightened and looked over my shoulder. "Geoffrey? Can you come here for a minute?"

From across the room, a man who looked so much like Deborah they could be twins joined us. The same man who'd followed her into the room earlier. As before, he moved languidly, as if he had all the time in the world. "What?"

"Aly, Olive, this is my charming brother Geoffrey."

"Geoff." He grunted rather than speaking his name.

"It's nice to meet you," I said, wondering what he had to do with any of this.

"Have you seen the pink flowered tea service? I put it in a box." To us, Deborah explained, "Geoffrey was watching the cashbox when I stepped outside."

"Full set? Ugly pink flowers?"

"It's beautiful," I said.

He shrugged. "I sold it to Lindsay. She said it was on hold for her."

My heart plummeted into my toes. Olive rested one hand on my shoulder, and Deborah sighed. "That was Aly's tea set."

He shrugged. "There are others. Aunt Miriam had loads of stuff."

"Yes, but I want that particular tea set."

"And I want to play for the Knicks. Life is full of disappointment."

The man in front of me stood a couple of inches above my eye level, and I wasn't particularly tall. I suspected that if he ever had dreams of playing basketball for a living, they disappeared about thirty years ago. Not that mentioning his height would help me get the tea service back.

One thing jumped out at me, though: if Geoff and Deborah were brother and sister, why was Deborah the only heir? Wouldn't most people split the money between them?

Unfortunately, nothing about Geoff's demeanor made me think he'd be up for sharing the family gossip. I'd have to see if Barry was willing to tell me anything later. First things first: I needed that teapot back. Without it, I had nothing.

"Do you know where Lindsay went? Is she still here?"

He shrugged again. "I'm not her keeper."

"Great. Thanks for all your help." I didn't try to hide my sarcasm.

Trying not to allow a frustrated sound to escape me, I swiveled on one foot and went to find the woman who'd stolen my teapot. To be honest, I'd been so stunned by the vision that overtook me, I barely remembered what she'd looked like. The tea set was another matter. I'd recognize that china pattern anywhere, even with my eyes shut.

In fact, that sounded like an excellent plan. Stopping in place, I shut my eyes and listened to the teapot, reaching for it with my powers. I'd never done such a thing before, but there was something strange about the items here.

For whatever reason, my Hail Mary worked. Something deep inside called me to the front door. Leaving Olive to check the other rooms of the mansion just in case I was imagining things that didn't exist, I raced for the entryway. There weren't nearly as many people here as in the rest of the house, and through the window, I glimpsed a familiar dark bob moving down at the end of the walkway.

I lunged for the door and yanked at the knob. Nothing happened. Someone had locked it. She was getting away! After throwing the deadbolt, I tried again. The door opened two inches, then cracked to a halt. The chain. I hadn't even seen it.

Argh! How many locks did one person need on their door? And why were they locked during a public estate sale?

Deborah or Geoff must have helped Lindsay make her getaway. It was the only explanation. Or... it was the bored teenager videoing me on his phone as I struggled to open the door. I resisted the urge to make a rude gesture.

Finally, I managed to get the dang thing open and lurched onto the porch. Lindsay was nowhere to be seen. Not knowing what else to do, I jumped down the steps and raced for the driveway. A car door slammed in the distance.

"Lindsay? Lindsay! Stop!"

In response, an engine roared to life.

Even though I still couldn't see her, I moved toward the sound, trusting the pull of the tea set to move me in the right direction. At the end of the line of cars, a red sedan pulled away. I ran toward it, yelling her name.

If Lindsay heard me, she gave no indication. She reversed in a circle. Realizing that I was never going to catch her, I paused long enough to pull out my phone and snap a picture of her license plate. Then I took off again, waving my arms and screaming all the way down the driveway.

At the street, I came to a dead halt and placed my hands on my knees as I gasped for air. There was no sign of the car. Lindsay was gone. My tea set was gone. And there went my only clue to Miriam's murder. Also, I needed to hit the gym more often.

Intellectually, I knew holding the teapot wouldn't necessarily make a difference in getting the police to believe poor Mrs. Peabody hadn't died of natural causes. The china wasn't likely to speak to anyone else. I doubted the Lunar Heights Police department employed any psychic officers.

Was there poison on the china? Someone probably washed it before putting it out to sell. My science classes didn't cover the half-life of poisonous residues on various surfaces. Would it vary by poison? Hmmm...

Not helpful. I shook my head to get back on track.

Would the tea set have fingerprints? Sure. Mine, Deborah's, Lindsay's, and probably Geoff's. That didn't seem super helpful. Oh, I couldn't forget Miriam's fingerprints, since she owned the set. Plus, whoever put it out for sale. That was a dead end.

Could there be DNA? Probably, but again, most likely from Miriam. Assuming it survived the dishwashing.

But over the past couple of months, I'd learned to trust my instincts, and something told me to get that box of china back. With a heavy sigh, I trudged back toward the house. Olive met me halfway.

"Any luck?"

"She's gone." The words came out as a sob.

"It's okay. We'll figure this out." She gave me a sympathetic smile. "It sounded like Geoff knows the woman who bought it. Maybe he can help."

"Yes!" A flash from the moments before the vision came back to me. "They definitely know each other. Or Deborah and Lindsay did, anyway. She kept calling her 'Debbie,' like she knew Deborah hated it. Deborah said Miriam wouldn't want Lindsay's mom to touch her stuff. Then Deborah lied, claiming she'd offered to sell me the tea set for fifty dollars, purely to irritate Lindsay. It cost two hundred."

"Interesting. So why did Lindsay go back to get it?" We turned and headed back up to the house. The sky had darkened, changing to reflect my mood. Dark clouds created a backdrop by the time we set foot back on the front porch.

"I wish I knew."

Geoff sat at the table where we'd left him. Deborah was nowhere in sight. Considering how unfriendly he'd been before, I wasn't excited to approach, but we didn't have a choice.

"Hi, Geoff. Do you know where Deborah went?"

"She's probably off taking a Xanax with a bottle of red

wine. My dear twin doesn't do well with things that resemble actual work."

"I take you it two aren't exactly siblings *and* best friends?"

After a moment, Geoff burst out laughing. "Considering she convinced Aunt Miriam to cut me out of the will, you could say that. Can I help you?"

As badly as I wanted to find my tea set, his words piqued my interest in a way I couldn't ignore. "She got you cut out of the will?"

"Yeah. I don't know how, so don't ask. It's been clear for the past few years that she's been slowly poisoning Aunt Miriam against me."

"That's terrible." I didn't want to minimize his pain, but I had a lot of questions that needed answers. "Did Deborah have any reason to be upset with Miriam? Do you know if they argued recently?"

"Not a clue," he said. "Neither of them talked to me much anymore. That's what happens when you become the black sheep of the family, you know. To be honest, I'm a little surprised they let me in here."

"Stop being overly dramatic," Barry said. He appeared out of nowhere, making me jump. "Miriam cut you out of the will because you were constantly asking her for money."

"That's not true! Look, we're family, and family should help each other when they're down."

"I agree completely. That's why when Miriam asked me to give you a job at my law firm, I jumped at the chance."

"Whatever. I have a job," Geoff grumbled.

"Out-of-work actor is not a job."

"I don't act! Why doesn't anyone ever listen to me?"

This conversation was getting further from proving that Deborah killed Miriam, so I struggled to bring it back around. "Look, I'm sorry about your issue with your aunt. There was some kind of mix-up with the tea set you sold to Lindsay. That was mine. Deborah was holding it for me back here."

"Oh, man! That sucks." He glanced down at the paperwork on the table and narrowed his eyes. "Sorry. Lindsay said Deborah was holding it for her, she paid, she left."

"How did she pay?" Maybe we could somehow get the address from her credit card? I didn't know how these things worked, but my friend Rusty might.

"Cash. Why?"

"No reason." I did know how cash worked. Too bad my powers didn't extend to touching cash and finding the address of the person who spent it. That would be cool. "Do you know where Lindsay lived?"

"No offense, but I'm not telling some random girl how to stalk poor Lindsay to get some china." Before I could argue, he said, "I don't see the appeal, personally. Want an espresso maker? She's got this killer machine that cost like eight Gs. Barry wouldn't let me have it."

"You could buy it, like anything else that's for sale," Barry said. "It's not up to me to give away Miriam's belongings or sell them at ninety-nine percent off."

"Can you help us get the tea set back?" I asked loudly. Both men jumped as if they'd forgotten I was there.

Barry pulled out his phone and excused himself like he couldn't get away from Geoff and this conversation fast enough. Part of me didn't blame him.

Olive said, "Deborah agreed to hold the set while Aly came to me to get her wallet."

"Sorry, chica," Geoff said. "No holds. No cash, no sale. If you'd paid for it, I'd give your money back but otherwise, go for the espresso machine."

Hmm. Every item in this place seemed to speak to me. Never had I been in a place so full of psychic noise, for lack of a better word. If Miriam had ever used the machine, it might be worth trying to get a vision. "Yeah, that sounds great. Can you point me at it?"

Geoff looked around the room, which had cleared out considerably since we arrived. "I'll do you one better. Let me lock the cash box, and I'll show you around."

"Do you really think anyone would steal from an estate sale?" I asked.

"I don't trust Deborah," Geoff said.

I didn't, either, but probably not for the same reasons.

"Is it stealing if she's the sole heir?" Olive asked. She had a point.

Geoff grunted. "She stole my entire inheritance. Aunt Miriam loved me when we were kids. Thought the sun rose and set on my shoulders. But somehow, over the past few years, Deborah convinced her that I just wanted her money. It's a load of garbage. I used to come by, do the landscaping, make her meals, fill the fridge. Then Deborah turned her against me, forced Miriam to drive me away." His brow furrowed as he looked around the room "Oops, sorry, the espresso maker is gone. It was right over there. What do you think about this serving platter?"

My first thought was that the item was rather gaudy and looked cheap. It was about a foot long, oval, with gold around the edges and a giant peacock in the middle. My second thought was that someone must've forgotten the decimal point in the price tag. Neither thought was helpful.

The platter weighed a ton. Holding it up, I tilted it into the light and let my eyes blur. A few weeks ago, I'd had some luck learning to scry, which helped me solve a murder. I didn't know if it was the lighting or the fact that I wasn't alone, but this platter showed absolutely nothing. Hoping I didn't look like a fool, I held it out in front of me and gripped the handles with both hands. Maybe I could induce a regular vision.

"What are you doing?" Geoff asked.

"Testing the weight," I said, as if it was the most obvious thing in the world. "You can't serve dinner on just anything. The dishes have to speak to you. To feel right in your hands."

"Uh, okay." He rolled his eyes. "Listen, I gotta jet. If you want to buy something, come get me."

"Well, that backfired," I said as Geoff left skid marks on the carpet leading to the doorway.

"He also left the cashbox, which is weird for someone convinced his sister is stealing," Olive pointed out.

"Stealing her own money," I added.

"Who's stealing their own money?" Barry asked. I hadn't noticed that this phone call ended. Interesting that a man with such a loud appearance could move so silently.

"Deborah, according to Geoff," I said.

"Oh, that's only the start of his conspiracy theories. He's convinced Liam hid treasure in this house. If I were you, I wouldn't put too much stock in anything he tells you. At one point, he tried to convince the entire town Miriam was senile."

He nodded at the platter in my hands. "Were you planning to buy that?"

I turned the item over and over, scrutinizing every inch. Closing my eyes, I counted the first ten elements before reopening them. The platter remained silent. "No. No, I just wanted to see if it was as ugly up close as from across the room."

Barry drew himself up stiffly. "That platter was a gift from me."

Silently, I cursed myself for my thoughtlessness. "I mean, it's really quite lovely. The teal on the rooster is very unique."

"I like the gold," Olive added helpfully. I could've kissed her.

Barry's face broke into a smile. "Relax, I'm kidding. Miriam loved roosters, had all kinds of stuff with images on them. It's quite the collection. A lot of it sold to an out-of-state collector, but they didn't want this one."

"Out of state? How many items did you sell to collectors outside of New York?" What if I needed to track them all down somehow? Solving this thing could take months.

"Just the roosters," he assured me. "Olive, I'm sorry, but I came to tell you that something's come up. I won't be able to go through the rest of the artwork with you until after lunch. Would you like to explore on your own for a bit or leave and come back?"

"We'll stick around," Olive said without missing a beat.

The only thing better than getting invited to snoop around this place all morning looking for clues was doing it without a representative of the estate watching. Unfortunately, we didn't have all morning—we still needed to find Lindsay. But if anything else here could help me prove Deborah killed Miriam, I needed to find it. Lindsay was probably going to her home, and she would still have the tea set if we found her in a few hours. Also, we didn't know where she lived.

Olive and I went from shelf to shelf, one piece of furniture to the next. I picked up a few books and paged through them, but nothing happened. Olive also touched the occasional object. After a few minutes, she put a black sticker on an antique radio.

"Tagging stuff you want?" I asked.

"Barry asked me to use these stickers for items that didn't belong to Miriam and Liam."

Ah. Since the house was getting crowded, I only nodded my understanding. We continued through the rooms. I tried on jewelry, including a fabulous tiara I secretly wanted but didn't really go with my college student uniform of leggings. I pretended to cook, pretended to clean, mimed eating and drinking from different objects. We must've looked ridiculous to the other people wandering around, but no one said anything.

Finally, we found the chair from my vision sitting in an alcove off of Miriam's bedroom. It must've been moved for the sale, because this wasn't the room where I'd seen it the first time.

I sank down into it, both exhausted and excited. With a deep sigh, I closed my eyes. Inhale, exhale. Again. My fingers ran over the cloth, tracing the raised pattern.

A shroud came over my vision. It looked like a polar bear in a snowstorm. Nothing but a sea of blinding white. Buzzing filled my ears. White noise. A distant voice, so quiet I could barely make it out. "Help me."

No matter how I strained, that was it. No sights, not even the darkness inside my eyelids. No smells, although not all my visions had them.

With a groan of frustration, I opened my eyes and uttered a string of words you should never, ever say in a church. I didn't understand what I'd just experienced, but I thrived on logic, facts, and data. This vision was unlike any I'd ever had before. Not just a new data point on the chart of my powers, but a new page in the chart entirely.

"What's wrong?" Olive asked. "Did you see Miriam's death again?"

"No, it was like... radio static, almost," I said. "Like those old ghost hunter shows where someone hears a voice?"

"The ones that usually turn out to be a crossed wire?" she asked.

"Yeah, maybe," I said. "It sounded like someone was asking for help."

"Do you think Miriam was trying to contact you?"

"Maybe, yeah. But how? I'm not a medium."

"Have you ever tried to contact the dead directly?"

"Not since I was eleven. My friend Gabby and I found an old Ouija board in the attic."

She chuckled. "That doesn't count."

"I know," I said. "No, I haven't. It never occurred to me to, say, hold a séance and try to contact Katrina and ask questions about her death. It's hard to explain, but that doesn't *feel* like something I could do."

"Interesting. I think I know what you mean." Olive thought for a moment. "But what if Miriam had powers? She could be reaching out because she thinks you can help stop her killer."

Although I'd never thought about this sort of thing, Olive's words rang true. I wasn't a medium. Ghosts never spoke to me. I didn't see spirits. Objects, only. Visions, scrying. My powers were all in seeing things or events. But if Miriam had powers in life, who knew what she could do after she passed away?

"Interesting. That could explain it," I said. "Otherwise, I don't understand. First, this house is positively singing to me. Then, it all goes quiet. Okay, great. Maybe it was enough to have me in the house, ready to listen. I don't know. But the tea set's gone. Why isn't anything else triggering a vision? You can't tell me that was the only item in the house with powerful memories. Not when everything was so *alive* when we got here."

"That makes me think even more it was Miriam. She could have left when we met Deborah, not wanting to be so close to her killer." She spoke slowly, deliberately, more like she was thinking out loud than having a conversation. We continued moving through the house, stopping periodically to test something with our powers. "Then she returned to warn you?"

"You think that's why I can't see anything else? Because Miriam wanted to show me her killer, and now I know who it is?"

"Maybe. I guess we'll see. Let's let it percolate for a bit. Maybe we'll come up with another answer."

Speaking of answers, I remembered that she'd had a question for me when I went to borrow the money for the tea set. "What were you going to ask me earlier?"

"Oh! Thanks for reminding me," Olive said. "There's a wall safe in Liam's old office. That's the room where Barry and I were looking at the paintings. I started thinking, and I wondered if maybe you could open it."

How the heck would I do that? Melt the lock? "I wish I could tell you that I carried hydrochloric acid on me at all times."

"Not like that, silly," she said. "I thought you could use your powers. See if touching it gave you a vision of someone using the combination. Just an idea."

Oh. Well, that made a lot more sense. I'd actually tried something like that once before, hoping to glean my deceased professor's computer password from her keyboard. It hadn't worked, but a lot of experiments initially failed. Like, penicillin.

"Are we supposed to be breaking into the Peabodys' private stuff? There could be all kinds of stuff in there. A will, jewelry, passports..." Now that I'd started listing things, I couldn't think of any way that opening the wall safe wouldn't get us arrested.

Olive spared a glance at the doorway. "Barry wants to open it. He went to call his secretary for the combination. It should be in his files. I just thought we'd help him."

"Sure. Why not?"

She led me back up the stairs, to the room where they'd been working. A practically life-sized portrait of an old man on the wall had been shifted to reveal a metal square behind it.

"Is that painting stolen?"

"No, that's Liam. He had it commissioned a couple of years before he died. Barry doesn't remember a safe on the wall before that, but he admits he didn't spend much time in this room while Liam was alive."

Interesting. Okay. I took a deep breath, mentally reciting the first ten elements of the periodic table to settle my nerves. Closing my eyes, I placed my fingers on the cool metal dial next to the handle that opened the safe. I spun it around once, twice, then back. Nothing happened.

Since I usually needed to use an object before I got a vision, I input my old locker combination from high school. Three right, all the way around, nineteen left, ten right.

Nothing happened.

"Sorry," I said. "Either opening the safe wasn't momentous enough for Liam to leave any sort of lasting impression, or my powers don't work that way."

"It's okay. Just thought we'd try. You never know."

Too bad the safe wouldn't open because if we found, for example, a new will cutting Deborah out, that would help establish her motive. Or if someone left a bottle of poison with Deborah's fingerprints in there, that would be super helpful.

We left the office to search the rest of the upstairs for any evidence we could find.

The next door in the hallway opened onto a bathroom. Olive closed it without entering. Good call. If there was a vision of Miriam to be had in that room, I wasn't desperate enough to go looking for it. We moved on.

Next, we found a small library. Geoff stood close to the only wall not covered with books. As we watched, he knocked, listened for a moment, then knocked again. Guess he hadn't given up on his conspiracy theories after all. That explained why he'd come to the sale. After engaging a silent look, Olive and I moved on.

Once we got out of his earshot, I whispered, "Could someone be suppressing the psychic energy on the objects? Is that even possible?"

"Let's just say, for now, it's probably not impossible. This year has had you really reconsidering what you thought you knew, right?"

She spoke the truth. From learning that psychics existed in the first place to the realization that not only did I have psychic powers but so did my nephew—and, oh yeah, a powerful witch who may or may not be his aunt was out there looking for him—let's just say I'd suspended quite a bit of disbelief over the past two months.

The next door opened onto a bedroom twice the size of my spacious room at Kevin's. Wow. A gorgeous rose pink and gold sleigh bed dominated the space. On the far wall, thick, pink and gold brocade drapes covered what must be floor-to-ceiling windows, leaving the room in murky darkness. The carpet was so plush, I was glad to have worn flats. And on the floor beside the be—

The sight before me brought me to a screeching halt so fast, Olive walked into my back. I screamed, but not because of her. One hand flew to cover my mouth, holding in the contents of my lunch, which suddenly desperately wanted to make a reappearance.

"Aly? What's wrong?"

I couldn't speak. Couldn't breathe. Shakily, I pointed at the body lying on the rug.

CHAPTER SEVEN

Olive rushed past me toward the body while I dug in my bag for my phone. She dropped to her knees and started feeling for a pulse. We needed to call 911! I couldn't believe we'd been in this house at least an hour, with people traipsing in and out, and no one noticed a dead woman lying on the floor in the upstairs bedroom.

Who was she? What was she doing here? She looked about the same age as Deborah, which put her in her late forties or early fifties. As far as I knew, no one lived with Miriam, but maybe she was an aide or someone here to help with the sale? The woman wore a pair of gray leggings and a pink sweater. I didn't remember seeing anyone in that outfit downstairs, but I probably wouldn't have noticed while they were walking around.

Her head was twisted to one side, and her open eyes stared blankly into the distance. There was no way to know how long she'd been lying there, or how long she would have stayed in that position if we hadn't stumbled in here. Poor thing.

Two sets of feet pounded down the hall toward the

bedroom. Was one of them the killer? Should we hide? Before I could come up with a plan, I raced around the bed and dove for the ground. Not a great hiding spot, but all I had on short notice. My shoulder whacked the nightstand, sending it toppling to the ground. Ow. "Olive! Hide!"

"It's okay, Aly. This isn't real." Olive's voice was surprisingly calm under the circumstances.

"I wish it weren't, but all the evidence says otherwise." I sighed. "I'm so sorry. No one ever found dead bodies before I moved to Shady Grove, and now it seems like they're everywhere."

She cleared her throat and stood, brushing off her hands. "No, I mean—the person isn't real. It's a dummy."

Before my brain could finish processing her words, the footsteps moved closer. "What?"

"As soon as I touched it, I got a vision of Deborah's brother. My powers don't work on people. Also—"

A female voice from behind us interrupted. "Is everything okay? We heard someone scream."

Deborah and Geoff stood in the doorway. They stopped dead when they realized what we were looking at.

"Darn it, Geoff! I told you to put that away."

"This is yours?" I asked.

Deborah said, "Geoff likes to play with dolls."

"I don't play with *dolls*, I am a Property Master," Geoff said loudly. "Deb never gets that right. I make props and masks for horror movies. This here is Bessie. She's some of my finest work. Looks real, doesn't she?"

She did look real. Even up close, Bessie's skin looked lifelike. She had short dark hair and perfectly placed features. Her eyes were closed, her head twisted unnaturally to one side. But now I saw that Geoff easily twisted it back into place.

"You fooled me," I said.

"Don't call me Deb," Deborah snapped at the same time. "Why is Bessie here instead of at your apartment where she belongs?"

"I was working on her here, with Miriam," Geoff retorted. "I needed the space. Then the job fell through, and it hurt too much to come pick her up. Sorry."

Now that my heartbeat had slowed to its normal place, I wondered if "Bessie" had seen anything while she was here. Maybe I could get a vision from her. Not that I knew how on earth to do that. Especially not with Deborah and Geoff bickering three feet away.

"It's grotesquely beautiful," Olive said.

Geoff glared at her. "She. Bessie is a she."

"Right. Sorry. She is beautiful," Olive said. "Do you want us to take her back to Missing Pieces with us? I can put her in the van before anyone else wanders up here."

"That would be great," Deborah said.

At the same moment, Geoff said, "No! Bessie's not for sale. I'll take her home. She can ride shotgun."

"I'm not riding in the back," Deborah snapped at him. "Your car only has two seats. Put her in the trunk."

"You drove together?" I asked. That seemed surprising, considering their relationship.

"I made her pay me fifty bucks."

Deborah rolled her eyes. "I'm starting to regret that decision. But he's the only family I have left. Unfortunately."

Things were getting more and more awkward, so I turned to pick up the nightstand I'd knocked over. The drawer had come out, skittering under the bed. Kneeling down, I reached for it. My fingers closed around a book. Great. What else had I spilled?

I threw myself flat on the ground as the bickering continued above me. Only the book, apparently, so I put it back on the now-upright nightstand just in time to hear Deborah shriek, "It's wearing my sweater!"

That was our cue. Olive and I mumbled some non-words that got ignored and left the two of them alone.

As soon as we got down the hall, Olive whispered, "Looks like we got out just in time."

"Well, sure, but we still don't have any clues." I chanced a look back at the room over my shoulder. "You don't think she'll kill him, too, will she?"

"Doubt it. Too many witnesses. Are you okay?"

I shook my head. "I'm going to wander outside for a few minutes to clear my head."

"Sounds good. I'm going to go review the few remaining images Barry wanted me to look at so we're not here all night. Shout if you need anything."

Outside, I paused on the step to take it all in. The sweeping grounds of the estate extended so far in every direction, I couldn't see the street or any of the neighbors. Must be lonely, living here without anyone else to talk to.

After breathing in the fresh air for a few minutes, I called the police. They needed to know what happened to Miriam.

"Lunar Heights Police. How can I help?" A very perky-sounding woman answered the phone, cracking bubble gum. I imagined her with big hair and blue eye shadow up to her forehead.

"Hi, my name is Aly Reynolds, and I'm calling about Miriam Peabody," I said.

She tsked. "Oh, poor thing. You didn't know? Miriam had a heart attack a few weeks ago. What happened? Did she call you out for having an emotional support ficus? That happened to me a few weeks ago."

"Uh, no, but thank you for asking." Were emotional support plants a thing? Better to move on. "Actually, I'm calling because I don't think she had a heart attack. I have reason to believe she was murdered."

Her voice hardened instantly. "If this is a joke, you should know it's a crime to file a false police report. You could face up to six months in jail."

I forced myself not to sigh into her ear. This wasn't the first time police threatened to lock me up, and it probably wouldn't be the last. "I understand. Listen. I believe she was poisoned. I found this tea set at her estate sale, and I swear that if you test it, you'll find something toxic on it."

"I can't promise you anything, honey, but if you bring it in, I'll pass your tip along to the detective."

"That's the problem. I don't have it."

"Where is it?" Her tone suggested I was losing her fast.

"Well, someone else bought it. But I'm sure you could get a warrant and find out where she lives."

"You've been watching too much TV." The woman laughed. "Sorry, dear. Tell you what. If you find the tea set, bring it on in. Meanwhile, give my regards to Deborah. I'm Gloria. That's Officer Gloria Tanner. Deborah and I spin together when she's in town."

Wonderful. My evidence was gone, and my suspect was friends with the cops. (Was she still a suspect if I knew she did it? Things to ask Kevin later.) She may not be a homicide detective, but Gloria served as gatekeeper for the Lunar Heights Police Department, and I didn't have a key. It wasn't worth arguing with her. Not until I tracked down the missing teapot.

"Okay, then, I'd like to report a stolen item," I said. "I'm at Miriam's estate sale now, and someone named Lindsay took off with a tea service that had my name on it."

"Lindsay Grant of the Long Island Grants?"

"Um...maybe?" No idea who the Long Island Grants were, but she might be one of them. How many Lindsays lived around here? "Short black hair, haughty air, steely gaze?"

"That's her, all right. Her parents own the largest house on Long Island. You're saying she stole a tea set? That sounds awfully far-fetched to me."

"Sort of," I said. "They were holding it for me, but she came along and paid for it before I could get my wallet from my friend."

The woman on the other end of the phone snorted. "Sorry, sweetheart, that doesn't count. We're pretty slow around here, but call me when you've got a real crime to report."

I bit back a snotty retort, since I really did want the police to help. Just as soon as I found some evidence. Before hanging up, I forced myself to thank Gloria politely.

Then I immediately dialed someone who could give me more than condescending comments: my best friend Rusty. Besides being extremely useful when I'd first discovered my psychic powers, Rusty had been at my side when I'd solved the first murder in Shady Grove in twenty years. More importantly, he was now training to be a private investigator, and he could help me locate Lindsay if I texted him the picture of her license plate.

"How is the most wonderful man I know?" I asked when he answered.

"Aren't you having dinner with Sam? You should ask him," he shot back.

"Heh. Valid. He's pretty great."

"Why are you buttering me up?"

"I need a favor. How's the PI training going?"

"Excellent! I've learned that Ayesha always takes her coffee black, and Dwayne wants chocolate milk in his." He sighed. "But I'm not supposed to tell anyone that. He calls it a 'How Now Brown Cow.' Which I'm totally giving to Julie for the coffee shop. Sorry. Anyway, what's up?"

Keeping my voice low in case anyone from the house should come outside, I explained about the humming, how it stopped, and the tea set. Finishing up, I said, "I need an address for Lindsay Grant, if you can. Apparently, she's from Long Island."

"Can you tell me anything else about her? Description? Job? What kind of car she drives?"

"Oh! Yes! She nearly ran me over."

"Way to bury the lede," Rusty said. "Are you okay?"

"Fine. She missed. And I got a pic." I gave him the rest of the details, then told him everything I knew about Deborah as well. "An address for her might come in handy, although at least I know where she works."

"Consider it done. Probably. Text me the plate. I'll ask my boss to help."

"Thanks, Rusty." I sent the image before finishing my sentence. "You're the best."

"Don't I know it. Tell Sam to keep you out of trouble for me."

I chuckled. "Yeah, sure. You tell Doug to keep you safe."

Doug was Rusty's live-in boyfriend and one of the three members on the Shady Grove police force. His uncle was the sheriff, who hated me. All because I wouldn't let him pin a murder on Olive to make the mayor look good. I know, I know. How dare I?

"Love you, Aluminum."

"Shove it, Ruston."

"At least I'm named after my cool British grandfather, not tin foil."

Ouch.

A click behind me made me spin around. Barry sat on a bench just outside the entrance to the gardens, lighting a cigarette. When he saw me, he flushed and closed his fancy flip-top lighter, setting it beside him. "A nasty habit, I know. I'm too old to stop now."

"It's not my place to tell you how to live your life." Especially now, when I had bigger fish to fry. "I tried to call the police."

"Gloria wasn't helpful, was she?" he asked, as mildly as if he commented on the weather.

"So you've met her."

"Everyone knows Gloria. Big eyes, big smile, big sense of self. Will never be promoted to Investigator because she can't keep her mouth shut, but she's pretty good at what she does."

"That explains why she wouldn't take my statement. She was sure Miriam died of natural causes."

"Oh, Gloria is never wrong. About anything. Just ask her."

He seemed composed, calm. I suspected he knew more than he was telling me. It couldn't be a coincidence that Olive and I had been called here to check the art and stumbled into a murder. "Hey, if I tell you something, do you promise not to say anything to anyone?"

"I'm a lawyer. If you want to hire me, anything you say is confidential. I couldn't reveal it, even if called to testify."

"I'm pretty sure I can't afford to hire a lawyer, even if I needed one."

"Well then, let me tell you a story. Have a seat." He

patted the bench beside him, and I sank down gratefully. "I've known Olive since she was in college, did she mention that?"

I shook my head.

"When we met, my son had been accused of doing some terrible things. I'll spare you the details. She proved he didn't do it by establishing that a shirt left at the scene by the perpetrator belonged to someone else. That person wound up confessing, which earned her my eternal gratitude."

"She helped me a lot since we met," I said. "I would do anything for Olive."

"You cleared her name of murder once, didn't you?" When my face registered surprise, he said, "I read all about the case in the paper at the time."

Other than Olive, only a handful of people knew about my powers. Most of them witnessed me having a vision before I told them. The idea of everyone knowing, seeing me as different made me uncomfortable. I wanted to ask what Barry knew about me, but I couldn't bring myself to say the words. Instead, I surveyed the gardens, waiting for him to continue.

My patience paid off after about three minutes. "When Miriam died and I had reason to think that foul play was involved, I called Olive first. I hoped she could use her gifts to help me find the truth."

That made me sit up straighter. "So you didn't really think the paintings were stolen?"

"No, I did. Liam had quite the reputation, and he always lived beyond his means, even with his family money. But when I called, I asked Olive if she could somehow see how Miriam died. She told me that she had an assistant now, who was as talented as she was...but in a very different and potentially more useful way."

"You knew what I could do before I got here." Now that I thought about it, it made perfect sense. Olive didn't need me to watch her work.

He nodded. "It was possible I was wrong, of course. I didn't want to say anything that might influence you. After all, I don't know how it works."

"Nothing you told me could change what I see," I said. "I think. This is still new."

"I understand. Please forgive me for keeping my silence. I had to try for Miriam. I couldn't let it go."

I patted his hand awkwardly, just for a second. "I get it. If I can help, I'm happy to. What made you think Miriam didn't die of a heart attack?"

"Miriam was in perfect health. Never even a cold as long as I've known her. It was as if germs were afraid to invade her body."

If that was his entire reasoning, he was lucky I had psychic powers. "I'm no doctor, but I'm not sure it works that way. Besides, I thought Deborah came up here frequently to take care of Miriam. Is that not true?"

"Miriam wasn't sick. Deborah thought she was lonely. They played cards, they talked, they baked, they played tennis together twice a week."

And then Deborah killed her. What a terrific niece, I didn't say.

"You said Deborah *thought* she was lonely. You mean she wasn't?"

"Miriam was surrounded by people who cared about her." The soft smile on his face suggested he was one of them.

"How long have you known Miriam?"

"Oh, years. I drafted Liam's will, you know. Did both of them at the same time. When Liam passed back in '08, I served as his executor. Helped Miriam tie up the loose ends." He paused and blinked a few times. "I'm going to miss her. You probably think I'm making up conspiracy theories because of my grief."

"Not at all," I assured him.

"You believe me? You think she was murdered?"

"I do, one hundred percent. I had a vision," I said. "I saw the whole thing. Deborah and Miriam were sharing a pot of tea. Deborah didn't touch hers. When Miriam sipped from her cup, she tasted something off. Then she collapsed."

Barry gasped. "You're sure?"

"I am. Why do you seem surprised?"

"Even though I suspected, I didn't want to believe anyone would hurt her. I was hoping you would call me a foolish old man and head back to Shady Grove."

I shook my head. "Wish I could. Do you know if the police did an autopsy?"

"They did an initial examination and determined that she died of natural causes. I don't know if they did any tests, but they probably wouldn't have thought to look for poison. Not to find out how a seventy-four-year-old woman died in her own home."

"I'm sure you're right. Unfortunately, I didn't see the poison, so I don't know what it was. There wasn't a conveniently labeled bottle sitting on the coffee table." I gestured at the garden. It was at least a football field long, with a mass of bright and glorious flowers blooming. I couldn't identify most of them. "It could have been anything. Miriam could've grown it right here."

"I doubt that."

"Why?" His certainty surprised me.

"Miriam hired a team of gardeners to take over that plot about ten years ago. She loved the work but couldn't manage the long hours kneeling in the dirt anymore. Still, she ruled over them with an iron fist. All-natural everything. We'd...I mean, she...hand-selected the plants, watched over them while they worked, wouldn't even allow pesticides. She never would've forgiven them if her dog or one of the neighborhood kids ate something that made them ill. I don't see her growing anything toxic."

"So we're back to square one," I said.

"Not exactly," he said gently. "Now you know she was murdered. You also know it was poison. All we're missing is the bottle."

"Silver linings. We also know who did it. Just can't prove it."

Barry shook his head, still looking out at the roses. "I never would have guessed Deborah would kill her aunt. She seemed so devoted to her. You're sure?"

"Yeah, but I don't have any real evidence," I said. "Geoff sold the tea set that triggered my vision. When I arrived, the items in the house were humming at me. But I walked around, and I'm not getting anything anymore."

"Has that happened to you before?"

"Only once, when the item was scrubbed," I said. "Could Deborah know enough to do a cleansing?"

Barry shrugged. "It's 2021. Anyone can know almost anything, thanks to Google."

"Fair point."

"More importantly, she has access to the house. Miriam gave her the alarm code decades ago. Assuming she knew what she was doing, she would have been able to easily come and do whatever was necessary long before today."

The house was probably a dead end, then. Deborah had

been inside, alone with Miriam's stuff for weeks. If Miriam was trying to send me a message, she might not be able to do it with Deborah physically on the premises. I needed that tea set. Time to find Olive so we could figure out our next steps. She would probably be done reviewing the paintings by now.

Barry put out his cigarette in what I'd thought was an old vase beside the bench. Maybe it was, but apparently, it doubled as an ashtray. He stood and started to walk toward the house when something glinted on the bench beside me. I called to him as I picked it up.

"Yes?" he asked.

"You forgot your lighter." It was big, heavy. Silver, embossed with a large BR on each side. Instead of making him walk back to the bench, I took it over to him. I needed to go to the house, anyway.

"Thanks," he said, "I'm always losing this. Maybe people should stop returning it."

"You could always get another."

"True, but this one has sentimental value." He sighed and put it in his pocket. "Ah, well. Let me know if I can help in any way. Excuse me, I just remembered I have to make a call."

I made it ten feet away when Barry called my name, bringing me to a halt. "What do you need?"

"I just remembered something extremely important."

"Something more important than Miriam getting killed?"

"Not more important, related. Deborah's leaving the country tomorrow morning," Barry said. "She's got a flight out of JFK just after ten o'clock. If you can't convince the police she killed Miriam by then, she'll get away with murder."

CHAPTER EIGHT

An hour later, Olive and I still hadn't found any hard evidence that Deborah had killed her aunt. This was so frustrating! Twice, I'd been involved in investigations recently, and both times, figuring out the killer's identity was the hardest part. It hadn't been necessary to convince the police that Earl Parker and Professor Zimm were murdered: few people hit themselves in the back of the head or buried themselves in the woods.

I was sitting on the stairs in the foyer with my head in my hands when the front door opened. A familiar voice said my name. When I looked up, everything got brighter. Sam Green stood there, highlighted by sunlight that created a halo effect. Even without it, his light brown hair and crooked smile made him glow in my eyes.

Oh, I had it bad for this man.

"Hey!" I didn't even try to contain the smile on my face. I jumped to my feet. "What are you doing here?"

"Mom called. She knew we had plans later, but she said if I was free now, I should come pick you up."

"Your mother is a saint." I glanced around and lowered my voice. "Did she tell you what happened?"

"I got the highlights. How can I help?"

"Rusty should call any minute with Lindsay's address. He can't do the work himself, so he had to ask his boss for help. I'm not sure how long that will take. Once we hear from him, we go talk to her about tea set stealing."

"Sounds good. Let me go say hi to Mom," he said.

We found Olive upstairs in the room where she'd spent most of the morning, looking at the computer with Barry. Liam had been quite the art collector, apparently, but he didn't seem to have been willing to pay for those valuable paintings. We were taking about a half dozen pieces to the store for sale, and the rest were going back to their rightful owners.

When Sam and I entered, she looked up. "You ready? I'll just grab my coat."

"You don't have to stop what you're doing," I said, after introducing Sam to Barry.

"We're looking at pictures of Barry's grandkids," she said.

Barry said, "Yeah, we're all done here. Thank you both for all your help."

"It was my pleasure," Olive said.

"Don't thank me yet," I grumbled. "I lost the only piece of evidence we had."

"And now we'll find it." Olive picked up her purse as she spoke and slung it over one shoulder. "Let's go."

"What do you mean 'we'?" I asked. "Don't you have reservations and a show tonight?"

"Aly, I can't leave you alone to figure this out."

"A, I'm not alone. I have Sam now. Thank you, by the

way, for calling him." She smiled at me, and I continued. "And B, those tickets cost more than I make in a month."

"Two," Sam muttered. "I got the good seats."

"Two months?!" I exclaimed. "Olive, you're going. You can't just toss them away. Don't argue. Sam and I are waiting for Rusty to find Lindsay's contact info. We'll go from there. But you can't miss the show."

"Are you sure?" She looked at her son. "I need you to swear on my life that you won't let Aly confront a murderer while I'm out."

"If there is any possible way to stop her, I'll take it," he said. "Scout's honor."

"You were never a Boy Scout."

He looked at me. "That's the problem with mothers. They know everything." To Olive, he said, "Mom, go. In fact, leave now."

"Okay, fine, I'll go. But text me if you find anything. Maria and I will pick you up after the show. If you get yourself killed, I'll never forgive you."

Finally, she got in her car to head to the city. We were alone. I walked over to Sam. "It's so good to see you again."

He wrapped his arms around me, and I rested my head on his shoulder. He smelled like cinnamon and happily-ever-afters. I allowed myself a moment to melt against him. From the moment we'd met, I'd had a crush on Sam. We even shared one glorious, heart-stopping kiss about a month ago.

Unfortunately, until I got my powers under control, I was afraid of getting involved with anyone. There was just no telling how I would react from getting too close to Sam or touching his...belongings. With a small sigh, I stepped back.

"It's good to see you, too," he said. "How do you feel?"

"Like there's a tornado inside me. I've got less than

twenty-four hours to prove Deborah committed murder before she disappears. Sorry for ruining the date you planned."

"Nothing is ruined. We'll find Lindsay," he said. "I'm at your disposal. What do you need?"

"Rusty's going to call me back. Meanwhile, let's make one more pass through the house."

Ten minutes later, Rusty came through like the star he was. The sale hadn't ended yet, but I'd seen more than enough. Address in hand, Sam and I set out to pay a surprise visit to Lindsay's home, thankfully only a few blocks away. Hopefully, she'd gone there after leaving the Peabody house, because I didn't have any idea where else to look for her. Spending the rest of the day on a stakeout didn't sound all that exciting, even with Sam.

After seeing Miriam Peabody's estate, nothing should have surprised me, but the Grant house was impressive in another way. All glass, new construction, right on the beach. Just the thought of what tiny fingers would do to smudge up those windows gave me a headache.

When Lindsay opened the door, she scowled at us. "What are you doing here?"

"We need the tea set!" I blurted out.

Sam poked me in the side as Lindsay started to swing the door shut. Panicked, I lunged forward. The glass and steel (who had a glass front door?) bounced off my foot. Ow. I gritted my teeth together, determined not to scream.

Steel was made of carbon and iron. Carbon was element six. C. Iron was element twenty-six. Fe. Fe fi foe fum... Was that why the giant in *Jack in the Beanstalk* said that? No. Element twenty-seven was cobalt.

The familiar recitation soothed me while Sam apologized to Lindsay over my head. Hmmph. Sure, I was being rude, but we were on a time crunch here. Tomorrow morning, Deborah would be getting on a plane and leaving the country forever. We needed evidence to stop her.

"Please, if you could give us just five minutes of your time, we need to talk to you," Sam said. "It's urgent."

Lindsay huffed but flung the door open and sauntered down the hall. Probably an invitation, so we followed a hallway tiled with what looked like glass cubes holding embedded sand and shells. Whoever designed this place must love the beach. The perfume she'd worn at the estate sale permeated everything. Part of me was afraid I'd leave here smelling like one of my mom's magazines.

At the entrance to the living room, Lindsay turned and crossed her arms over her chest. "What's so important?"

Since she didn't have a monopoly on rudeness, I flopped onto her tan leather couch. Oh, that was amazingly soft. Sam sat beside me, a reminder that we'd come here for a purpose.

"Listen, I know you really liked that tea set, but I did see it first. Deborah promised to set it aside so I could buy it. Geoff didn't know he wasn't supposed to sell it to anyone before I got back. I realize that probably doesn't mean much to you, but it's extremely important to me that I get that tea set back as soon as possible."

"Oh, that. I thought you were looking for donations to the Salvation Army."

Sam and I exchanged a look. She didn't remember meeting me a few hours ago? She wasn't listening when I asked for the tea set as she opened the door? Before we could say anything, Lindsay waved one hand airily. "Turns out my mom has almost the exact same one. I gave it to my nanny when I got back. She's having a yard sale or something."

"Didn't you spend two hundred dollars on it?" Since I rarely had two hundred dollars to my name, I couldn't imagine throwing something away that cost so much. Especially not after almost getting into a fistfight with a stranger for it.

Sam elbowed me. "I think what Aly means is, do you have her address? We'd like another chance to buy it."

"You want it that badly?"

"We really did love it," I said, taking Sam's hand. "It reminded me of the place where we had our first date. With our anniversary coming up, the memento would be so meaningful."

"That's sweet." Lindsay smiled tightly. "Hold on to that sentimentality before you become bitter and jaded by the real world. Like Geoff."

"You and Geoff... are a couple?"

"We used to be," she said. "But at some point, he became completely obsessed with money. He turned into a different person. He had a new scheme every week, always trying to get Miriam to invest in this or that. Constantly badgering me and Deborah for money. He wanted to search the house for cash, too. Convinced himself that Miriam had a stash of money or jewels or art, maybe? I don't even know. Liam liked to make up wild stories about all kinds of things: vampires and treasure and monsters and being a pirate. For some reason, this one stuck with Geoff. Eventually, his insistence that she let him search the house put a strain on my friendship with Deborah. Even after Geoff and I broke up, things never went back to normal between us."

"That's too bad." The sympathetic thing to say was probably to suggest they try to make up, but since Deborah was a murderer, Lindsay could do better in the friend department.

"Yeah. Geoff was so angry to find out he'd been cut out of Miriam's will." She laughed hollowly. "I didn't know how to tell him it was probably because he'd been trying to milk her dry for years."

Part of me desperately wanted to ask why she'd dated him, but that was way off-topic and none of my business.

"I hate to be a pain," Sam interjected, "but we don't have a lot of time. Could you possibly find your nanny's address for us?"

"And her name?" I added.

"Yeah, sorry," she said. "Her name is Crystal. Hold on. I'll tell you where to go."

Sam looked like he wanted to tell her where to go, but that wouldn't be helpful. Apparently, the address of Lindsay's nanny wasn't important enough to be included in her contacts app. We had to wait ten minutes while she looked up her accountant's phone number and called him to get the information. Before handing it over, she made us sign a non-disclosure agreement she printed from her phone. What did she think we were going to tell people? I may have rolled my eyes the entire time, but we read quickly and signed. There wasn't time to argue.

I didn't know the area at all, but the address said Long Island, so Crystal couldn't live that far away. She drove here every day. My phone was out, fingers already typing it into my maps app as Sam thanked Lindsay and hustled me toward the door.

Unfortunately, Long Island was bigger than I'd hoped. I thought my phone was just wrong when it said we were over an hour away, but then I double-checked.

Nope.

Long Island was not a misnomer. It was, in fact, a long

island, roughly seventy times the size of Shady Grove. Naturally, Crystal lived on the other side.

It took every ounce of restraint I had not to tap my fingers on the armrest the whole way. Sam drove as fast as he could manage, but he couldn't collapse space to get us there in thirty seconds. Still, when he stopped for gas, I almost had a meltdown.

It took me reciting the elements up to fifty-three to calm down, and by then, we'd almost reached our destination. It also helped that Sam handed me a burrito he'd picked up inside while paying. I hadn't eaten since breakfast. The whole thing could've tasted like shoe leather, but it vanished down my throat in three seconds flat, so I'd never know.

"There!" Sam leaned forward and gestured toward my window. "It should be right up there."

"Up where? We're at number thirty-seven. Crystal lives at sixty-four."

"She does, but look. Didn't Lindsay say Crystal was having a yard sale?"

Oh, fluoride. (I was trying not to swear.) Parked cars lined the street ahead of us as far as the eye could see. A trickle of pedestrians all led to the same house: a modest ranch painted baby blue, with a white picket fence around the outside. It looked like the occupants should have three-point-two kids and at least one dog.

"Hold on," Sam said. "I'll drive you up to the front and drop you off."

"Don't go too fast. What if someone is walking away with my tea set? It's in a big cardboard box. I hope they're not selling the pieces individually."

Obediently he inched along, not saying a word while I scoured the crowd. At the moment, more people were walking toward the sale than leaving. According to the flyer on a nearby lamppost, the same had started about twenty minutes ago. Small favors.

When we reached the bottom of the driveway, Sam let me out of the car and went to find a parking space. Larger items sat here: a couple of old bicycles, some skis, a train set that Kyle would love. With a sudden pang, I thought about how I'd love to be spending the day playing with him instead of chasing down yet another murder suspect. We hadn't spent a weekend apart since I moved in with him and Kevin.

By the time I made it to the entrance of the garage, Sam joined me. "Any luck?"

"I don't see anything, but I also haven't found Lindsay's nanny yet. She may know where to look."

"Can I help you?" a woman asked, appearing as if I'd summoned her. She was short, slight, with curly gray hair and a friendly, open face.

I jumped away from Sam guiltily. "Hi! I'm here to ask you about the tea set Lindsay gave you."

"Tea set?" The woman furrowed her brow. "I don't remember seeing a tea set."

"Are you Crystal?"

"No, dear." She smiled at me. "You want my daughter. She works for the Grant family. Crystal's inside. I'll get her."

The woman turned and went inside, and a moment later, a younger version of her appeared in the doorway, carrying a cardboard box. They could have been a "Before" and "After" advertisement for some miracle youth product sold by Gwyneth Paltrow.

After introducing ourselves, Sam explained why we'd come. He did much better with the talking part of investigating than I did. Crystal nodded along until he finished.

"That tea set had bad juju," she said. "I just finished cleansing it. We never could've sold it the way it was.

My blood went cold. "Cleansing it?"

She couldn't mean—She must have just washed the tea set, right? Would running it through the dishwasher take away the psychic impressions? She set the box on the folding card table where someone had set up a cashbox. "Yeah. The whole set needed it. Take a look, all the pieces should still be here."

Since I couldn't breathe, Sam dug into the box. One by one, he removed the tray, each of the cups, the sugar bowl, and the creamer. When only the teapot remained, he turned to look at me. I nodded, wordlessly. He removed it from the box almost reverently. Crystal looked at us like we were both part of some teapot-worshipping cult. If we didn't wrap this up soon, she'd toss us out of her garage.

Sam turned the teapot in his hands, examining it carefully. Unfortunately, without psychic powers, it didn't tell him anything. At least not that I saw. After a moment, he handed it to me. With shaking fingers, I reached out and touched it. I pretended to pour tea, then I mimed drinking.

Crystal watched curiously but didn't comment.

Nothing happened.

With wide eyes, I looked up at Sam. "Cleansed means it's been erased."

CHAPTER NINE

Erased! How could the vision in the teapot be erased? My mouth opened and shut, but no sound came out.

Intellectually, I realized that I couldn't show the vision to anyone else whether I held the teapot or not. Having it wouldn't necessarily convince the police of anything. At the same time, I'd really hoped to view the vision again. Maybe I'd have been able to pick up some other details, information that might have led to hard evidence. Now we had to hope for residue on a teapot that the police probably wouldn't agree to test in the first place.

I was starting to daydream about bringing Porter at the science lab a new romance novel so he'd help me learn to test for poison when Crystal spoke.

"Is something wrong? You wanted the set; this is it. Cash only."

"Thank you very much," Sam said. He pulled two twenties out of his wallet and offered them to her. "Is this enough for the tea set and the trains?"

"You're at a yard sale, not FAO Schwarz. Most everything costs three bucks. This is fine. Thanks." She snatched the cash, then turned away.

Sam put one arm on my back and steered me down the driveway, toward the car.

"Thank you," I said once I put my disappointment aside enough to speak. "I didn't mean to lose it back there."

"It's okay, I get it. It's been a very stressful day," Sam said. "Hey, listen, I almost forgot, but do you want to go to the LaMonica Museum tonight?"

Immediately, I caught his real meaning. "You want to break into Deborah's work to look for clues the night before she skips town? I'm not sure I've ever liked you more."

His cheeks turned pink. "Well, no. They're having an event. Mom mentioned it on our way out of the mansion. We could ask people about Deborah, try to get some information. At the very least, we might talk her into giving us some dirt about Lindsay and Geoff's relationship."

Oh, yeah. In all the commotion with my tea set, I'd completely forgotten about Deborah inviting us to the abaci exhibit. "I like the way you think. Too bad she probably won't be there for us to talk to her."

"You never know," Sam said. "Depends on how much she loves math. But if she's not, we can check her office. If she's emptied it, we can use that fact to convince the police to get a warrant to search her apartment. Or to take Deborah in for questioning tomorrow morning before she gets to the airport."

According to my phone, it was already after seven-thirty, and the museum closed at nine on Saturdays. As I continued reading, my stomach plummeted. "It says it's sold out. We can't go."

"Not a problem," he said. "Barry gave Mom two tickets for us."

A squeal of joy escaped me. "I could kiss you!"

"An excellent idea." He smacked his lips dramatically. Leaning in, he planted one on me in an overly exaggerated fashion, leaving me giggling hysterically. Kissing Sam was good for my soul.

When I calmed down, I asked, "What's the dress code? I've got clothes for tomorrow in my bag, but nothing fancy. I wasn't sure I'd be staying over."

Sam shrugged. "What you're wearing is probably fine. They sell student tickets. Most college students aren't going to own anything black tie. Besides, it's a modern math museum. Nothing old and stuffy."

"True. We're going to look at abaci. Which is a super fun word. Abaci."

"You're cute when you're silly."

Good thing we'd been at the sale as representatives for Missing Pieces, or I might have shown up in my college student/nanny wardrobe of second-hand designer leggings and a hoodie. My black shirt and gray-blue pants (that were actually yoga pants but looked like dress pants—shh!) with a long red sweater should be okay.

"Okay. Let's go be nerdy."

WHATEVER I EXPECTED, the LaMonica Museum wasn't it. Colorful geometric tiles covered every inch of the outside. It looked like it was made of Legos, but in a good way. Nothing like any art museum I'd ever visited, but way more interesting.

Sam squeezed my hand as we approached. "I'm getting excited already."

Being here with him, geeking out together over our

shared interests? Absolutely the highlight of my month. "Me, too. I wish we weren't just here to solve a murder."

"When I'm with you, it's never 'just' about anything as mundane as murder."

His words sent a thrill through me.

The abaci exhibit was housed on the third floor. According to the map I grabbed from the entrance, the staff offices sat one floor above. The map also told me that we one hundred percent needed to come back when we had more time. This place looked amazing.

"Polypaint Patterns!" Sam read over my shoulder excitedly. "Da Vinci's Lesser-Known Inventions? A room about Galileo. This is the greatest place ever! How did I not know it was here?"

"You didn't know? Careful, or they'll make you return your math nerd cred."

Sam pulled himself to his full height and stuck his nose in the air. "I'll have you know that I was the first Shady Grove High Mathlete ever to get a perfect score three competitions in a row."

"That's so hot." I grinned at him. I wasn't being sarcastic, and we both knew it. "The only surprise there is that Shady Grove High had enough students to create a Mathletes team."

"It was mostly kids from Willow Falls."

Our flirty banter ended when we turned the corner onto the third-floor landing and spotted a sign for the exhibit. Sam looked as giddy as a kid in a candy store, and his excitement was contagious.

We were having so much fun that I almost forgot we weren't on a real date until we turned a corner and saw Deborah speaking with a small group of people. She spoke animatedly, and they all nodded along with interest.

"There she is!"

"Are you sure about this?" Sam asked. "Maybe there's a better way to gather evidence."

"A better way than talking to our primary suspect? Come on, we'll be fine. She wouldn't attack us in the middle of the museum. Especially because she has no reason to suspect we know anything. It's not like I plan to accuse her right here, in front of everyone."

"I'd like that in writing, please."

He seemed loath to leave the display of Mesopotamian abaci, so it wasn't entirely clear where his reluctance came from. "Are you worried about my safety or wanting to stay and nerd out a bit longer?"

"Can't it be both?"

"It can," I said, "but you have to decide quickly what you want to do. She just spotted us."

In response to my wave, Deborah approached. She'd changed after leaving the estate sale, out of her somber clothes and into a bright skirt with colorful triangles that reminded me of the museum's exterior.

"Aly! Sam! You made it!"

"I wouldn't miss a show like this for anything," Sam said. "I only wish I'd known in time to invite the other guys at school. Although, actually, I think I know some of these people."

Deborah's eyes twinkled. "Glad you're enjoying the exhibit."

"This place is awesome," I butted in.

"Thank you. I'm very proud of it. Want me to show you around?"

Although he was wary of confronting Deborah, Sam's face radiated glee at her offer. His joy was contagious.

The woman who showed us around the museum bore

very little resemblance to the person we'd met at the estate sale. That Deborah was doing a duty, helping her family, and working to wrap up her aunt's estate. This Deborah *glowed.* Like she was a plant, and the museum fed her sunlight. She thrived here in a way that only someone who truly adored their job could understand.

"It seems like you really love this place," I said as she took us up to the fifth floor.

"I do! It's my happy place. Whenever I'm sad or frustrated or anything, I come here. Most people get their stress from work, but not me. I love my job. I'd work here for free."

"Well, the good news is, now you can." Faking embarrassment, I bit my lower lip and glanced away. "I'm sorry, Deborah, that was insensitive. I shouldn't have said anything about Miriam's money."

"No, it's okay," she said. "You're not the first."

"What do you mean?" Sam asked.

"From the minute Aunt Miriam died, I've been bombarded with requests for money. Old friends, old roommates, the museum, even my stupid brother. The poor woman has only been in the ground for a few weeks. Can't I grieve in peace?"

Sam clucked his tongue sympathetically. He was way better at undercover work than me. "That must be tough. Still, it must be nice to be able to pay off all your debts, right? I lay awake at night dreaming of the bank 'losing' my student loan information, and I haven't even finished my MBA yet."

Deborah forced a smile. "That would be nice. I got scholarships for school, I was very fortunate. Geoff and I didn't need to take out loans."

"I'm jealous," I said. She winced. "And no, I'm not about to ask you for money."

"Sorry. Force of habit."

"Is there anything you can do that would make it easier?" Sam asked. "Get away from it all?"

"I'm going to Thailand tomorrow," Deborah said. "Trip of a lifetime. That should help. A week in the sun surrounded by people who have no idea what I'm worth. I can't wait."

"Sounds like a dream," I said.

"It's exactly what I need right now. Actually, I'm sorry, that reminds me—I should go. I have a few things to wrap up in my office before I take off. The place is a disaster, and my boss will never find the paperwork she needs. It was lovely to see you again."

"You too," I said.

"I'm sorry for your loss," Sam called after her.

We watched as she turned and disappeared down a long hallway. A moment later, we heard the beeping of a keypad, and a door clanged shut behind her. So much for getting evidence from Deborah.

CHAPTER TEN

By the time we made it back to Sam's car, it was only around nine o'clock, but felt like midnight. I sank into my seat with a sigh, leaning my head back against the headrest as my eyes fluttered shut. A moment later, the driver's door banged shut. I turned my face toward him, but opening my eyes felt like too much effort.

He squeezed my hand. "You okay?"

I groaned in response. We still had nothing. Okay, well, slightly less than nothing. Deborah acted like a bereaved family member when Miriam's name came up, but of course she would. She hadn't burst into tears and confessed to everything, which certainly would've made my life easier. Although she'd mentioned her vacation, she didn't act like someone planning to skip town and never come back. (Not that I knew what a fleeing murderer looked like.) The way she talked about her job, she wanted to do it forever. Unless she was planning to open a similar museum in Thailand, the entire encounter perplexed me.

Other than the abaci, the visit to the museum was a total

waste of time. I couldn't think of a single way to stop Deborah from getting on that plane tomorrow morning.

The car's engine roared to life, and a moment later, a welcome flood of hot air blasted me from the vents.

"Ohh, thank you. Why was it so cold in there? Art doesn't need to breathe."

"Welcome to New York. People get so excited when the snow melts, they crank the A/C starting at about sixty degrees."

"That is both bananas and terrible for the environment." Sitting up, I smiled at him. "Thanks."

"For what?"

"For helping me feel normal."

"If talking to you is all it takes, it is absolutely my pleasure," he said. "Listen, it's been a long day. You're exhausted. Let's go back to my place and figure out our next step."

At that, I wiggled my eyebrows at him. "Oh, yeah? Go back to your place?"

His face turned red. "I didn't mean it like that. We'll hatch a plan."

His embarrassment was contagious. Now I felt stupid. Although we'd been flirty and kissy most of the afternoon, we apparently hadn't reached the "joking about being intimate" portion of our... relationship? Friendship. Whatever we were. "Sorry. Just trying to, well, be awkward, I guess."

He raised our still-linked hands to his lips. "No, I get it. I'd like to take things slowly, if that's okay with you."

Considering I was terrified of having a vision of him with other women if we got too close? Yes, that was absolutely fine. "Definitely. I just want to spend time with you."

"Me, too. But we've been running around all day. It's time to slow down and take a breather. We need to figure out how to convince the police that Deborah killed Miriam, and there's no point in you going back to Shady Grove tonight when we have so much to do here. We haven't even made it to Kevin's storage unit yet."

More than anything, that last comment gave me pause. I needed to get into my brother's unit, to go through Katrina's stuff while I could. But other things kept getting in the way, forcing me to push back the visit. I desperately wanted to go tomorrow morning.

There was only one problem. As much as I didn't want to head home, I had nowhere else to go. "No point, except I can't afford to stay in a hotel."

"You don't need a hotel. You can stay with me."

For the second time in about forty seconds, my hopes shot up. But I quickly dashed them. "Don't you have roommates?"

Sam was a post-graduate student living in New York City, so I didn't imagine for a second that he could afford to live in an apartment on his own. "Yeah, but two of them have already gone home for the summer. Lucky dogs had their last finals a week ago. Adam is around, but he'll be in the other bedroom."

"Other bedroom?"

"We have an apartment-style dorm. Two bedrooms, two beds in each. A shared living room, kitchen, and bathroom. You can sleep on the couch."

I could sleep on the couch of a shared living room where four guys routinely sat, along with who knows how many other people? I hesitated. As much as driving back and forth to Shady Grove didn't make any sense, I had my own bed there. No one had slept in it but me, no possibility of getting haunted by visions in the middle of the night.

Sam sensed my hesitation. "I get it if you don't want to. I know it's weird to stay with some guy you barely know."

"No. It's not that." I bit my lip, wondering how much to reveal. Sam knew about my powers, obviously. But sometimes, I liked to pretend that we were just a normal girl and guy who were hanging out and eventually going to fall in love and get a puppy together. Finally, I sighed. "I'm worried about sleeping on a surface other people have slept on."

He got it instantly. "Oh, right. The visions. I'm sorry."

"Yeah. I know, it's dumb."

"No, I should have realized. You haven't stayed in a hotel since your powers developed?"

I shook my head. "Mrs. Patel had to do a cleansing on my used car before I could drive it."

Sam snapped his fingers. "There you go! We'll cleanse my couch. There's a New Age store not too far from my dorm. They should have what we need. And for good measure, we can stop on the way back to the highway and get you a brand-new set of sheets."

My heart warmed. "You'd do that for me?"

"I'd do anything for you, Aly. Don't you know that by now?"

A smile spread across my face, matching the warmth in my veins at his words. "I didn't know, but me, too. I mean, I feel the same way. I mean—"

He leaned forward, pulling me in for a kiss. That certainly made me feel better.

While he drove, I texted Olive to head back home without me after *Hamilton* ended. I'd take the train up tomorrow after we stopped Deborah. According to the clock, she and Maria would be in the theater, so I didn't expect a response.

Soon, we were at Sam's building. Parking in Queens was no joke. Even at nearly ten o'clock, we spent almost an hour circling the block before we eventually squeezed into a place so tight, I wondered if he'd used magic to get the car in there.

The good news was, since we were twelve blocks away from his place, we didn't have to make a separate trip to get magic supplies. We'd have to walk by the store, anyway. Thanks to an extremely helpful employee named Starshine, we were soon back on the sidewalk with a bag full of everything we'd need for the cleansing, but it was too late to buy sheets. Next time, I'd bring my own.

Finally, we made it back to Sam's dorm. Only twenty minutes after eleven, my stuff was unloaded, the apartment was cleansed, and a very inviting bed was set up on the couch. We went over and over what we knew, rehashing every minute detail of my vision and every second of our interactions with Deborah.

"Hold on," Sam said after the second time I recounted the vision. "You said Miriam smelled almonds and tasted something bitter?"

"Yeah. She thought the tea was burnt. Does tea go bad?"

"It does when you put cyanide in it."

I blinked at him several times. "I'm sorry?"

"Cyanide smells like almonds, has a slightly bitter taste, and kills almost instantly."

That all tracked what I'd seen in my vision. "How would Deborah get cyanide?"

He shrugged. "It's New York. You can get pretty much anything. But also, it's in some pesticides and fruit pits. Didn't you say Miriam had a garden?"

"She did, although Barry made it sound like she

wouldn't use regular pesticides. I wonder if there's a way for the medical examiner to test for it."

"Probably not on what appears to be a routine heart attack case from last month. But knowing what poison Deborah used may make finding evidence easier."

By that point, I was falling asleep on my feet, so we went to bed. Although I'd been worried it would be awkward to sleep less than ten feet away from Sam, I barely managed to brush my teeth without falling over. As soon as my head touched the pillow, I was out.

My eyes flew open at the first rays of sun peeking over the horizon. Intellectually, I knew the human body needs sleep to function, but we'd lost five hours we couldn't afford. Sam was still asleep, and while I absolutely intended to wake him up, there was no point until I got sustenance for us both.

First, I got the coffee brewing. Then I turned my attention to breakfast. Turned out, Sam's apartment-style dorm came with a kitchen but no food. I borrowed his keys off the counter so I could get back in and ran out to the local deli for bagels, cream cheese, and lox. We were going to need a big breakfast to figure out how to stop Deborah from getting on a plane in about five hours.

"We should take the tea set to the police," I told Sam when he got up. "If Crystal only did a spiritual cleansing, any physical residue from the poison could still be there."

We took turns using the bathroom while the other ate. Before seven-thirty, we were once again in the car with the boxed tea set. Sam focused on the road, remaining silent while I pulled each piece out of the box and mimed using it, attempting again to induce a vision. Nothing worked. Finally, with a sigh of frustration, I shoved the entire box on the floor behind Sam's seat.

"One thing has been bothering me," Sam said after I slumped back into my seat and crossed my arms over my chest. "Why was Deborah being so helpful? Did she know Lindsay would get rid of the set or give it to her nanny? Why wouldn't she just tell you to move on?"

I let the words roll around in my head for a few minutes before answering. Earlier, I'd wondered the same thing myself. "I don't know. I've never encountered anything like this."

"Maybe she said it on purpose," Sam said.

"Why would she do that?"

"I don't know. To let you know that she knows about you?"

"So she was using the tea set like a trophy?" I asked.

"Or maybe she wanted us to spend all day trying to track it down while she skipped town. Keep us out of her hair."

"She sent us on a wild good chase." If that was the case, I was doubly grateful for Rusty's help. "Maybe we're reading too much into everything. Not everyone has powers. Maybe she has no idea what I can do, and it's just a tea set to her."

"Also a possibility."

Forty-five minutes later, we arrived at the police station. Since only the teapot had originally pinged my vision and I didn't know which cup Miriam drank from, I left most of the items in the box in Sam's car. We took the teapot inside and found ourselves talking to the same perky woman who'd answered the phone when I'd called yesterday, Gloria.

My heart dropped when I saw her. Deborah must be at the airport by now. Yesterday, Gloria laughed at my declaration that Miriam was murdered. Would today be any different? How did we get an officer who would take us seriously in the next twenty minutes or so? The whole way here, I'd prayed for a different officer on duty.

Unlike my vivid mental image, she was pretty ordinary-looking. Probably in her late fifties or early sixties, with short hair a shade of copper too bright to be natural. Brown eyes, no jewelry, little makeup. Big wad of gum, though.

She didn't seem any more inclined to believe someone murdered Miriam than the first time we spoke.

Finally, out of exasperation, I asked, "Is there a detective on-duty? Or a superior officer I could talk to? Someone else?"

"Honey, you're welcome to talk to the detective and my captain. They're one and the same, and he doesn't work on Sundays because of the Lord. You can come back tomorrow if you must speak with him."

Tomorrow would be too late, and if she'd been listening to me at all, Gloria knew it.

When I told her the tea set needed to be tested for traces of poison, she laughed. "This isn't the movies, sweetheart. We don't have time or money to do DNA tests on everything."

"But Miriam was murdered, I'm sure of it."

"Of course you are," Gloria said.

While she didn't want to believe she could be wrong about how Miriam died, Gloria did have a lot of thoughts about Deborah and Miriam. Thoughts she was happy to share. Never did I expect a police officer to have so many things to say about members of the community.

"Oh, I've known Miriam for *ages*," she said. "She used to babysit me back when she was Miriam Eggert. She'd never admit that to a soul now, of course, but Miriam wasn't born with money. She met Liam Peabody in high school, and he fell for her hard and fast. They told people it was love at first, sight, you know, but they failed to mention she was working as a carhop when it happened."

"I'm sorry," I said. "A what?"

"Carhop. A woman in booty shorts and roller skates who served food and drinks to people at the drive-in." She paused and examined me and Sam critically for a moment. "That's a movie theater where people used to sit outside in their cars and make out, pretending to be watching a film."

I bumped Sam with my hip. "Want to go to the drive-in later?"

"Smooth, dearie, but the last one closed years ago," Gloria said. "The internet and streaming, you know. Anyway, she was dating someone else at the time, but one look at Liam, and all Miriam could see was the dollar signs."

"Do you know anyone who might have wanted to hurt Miriam?" Sam asked, trying to move her back on track. I shot him a grateful look.

"Sure, everyone hates rich people. You know they stay rich by stiffing people, right? A few years before he died, Liam made a big deal about finishing the basement. Wanted to have a wine cellar put in, a movie theater, all kinds of stuff. Hired poor Lloyd Grant to do the job and never paid him." She paused, fanning herself with one hand. "Listen to me, getting all up in a tizzy. Anyway, that was years ago. Lloyd made his money converting old churches to condos long before that. He didn't need the money, only agreed to do it as a favor. He never forgave Liam for swindling him, though. Meanwhile, don't ask me how the basement turned out because they never invited anyone over to enjoy it. Stingy as a jellyfish."

I started to explain the difference between "stingy" and "sting-y," but decided I liked the sentiment. Interesting that

Lindsay would date Geoff after his uncle stiffed her dad, but he didn't seem all that close with the family. Maybe she thought the "Romeo and Juliet" thing was romantic. Gloria wouldn't know, so I didn't bother to ask.

"Deborah mentioned driving Miriam around a lot. Was she too cheap to pay for gas?"

"Nah. Miriam was blind as a bat, although she wouldn't admit it. She could've paid for a driver, but Deborah wanted to suck up to the old auntie to get her money," Gloria said.

"You don't believe their relationship was genuine?" Sam asked. "We talked to Deborah, and she seemed to really care about Miriam."

"Of course she did. That whole family, full of actors," she said. "Back in high school, the Peabody twins took the lead in every play. You should have seen them in *The Parent Trap.*"

"They played twin sisters?" I asked.

"Sure did. Deborah cut all her hair off; with makeup, you could barely tell the difference. Geoff's the only one who tried to make a go of the business full-time, poor thing. Luckily, the rest of them didn't, he's as broke as an old boxer's nose. Not that it should've mattered with Miriam's moneybags. But like I said, stingy. Saw no reason to share with her sister's kids while she was alive, even if they pretended to like her. My guess is she only picked an heir because she couldn't get buried with her fortune."

Gloria turned out to be an amazing wealth of information. Every word revealed another clue to the puzzle. Suddenly, I understood why Barry said she'd never get promoted.

Sam said, "Deborah and Geoff are twins. Why leave the money to one and not the other? Do you think Deborah was just that much better at sucking up?"

"She probably worried Geoff would fritter it all away. There wasn't a person in town he didn't hit up for an investment at one point or another." She pulled herself upright and glanced around. Then she adjusted her glasses and leaned forward, lowering her voice. "Between you and me, I heard Miriam was planning to change her will. Leave poor Deborah out in the cold, too, after she drove up here and took care of her on all her days off for the past eight years."

"That's terrible." Sam clucked his tongue sympathetically. "Why would she do that?"

"I don't know why rich people do anything," Gloria said with an exasperated sigh. "My guess is that her new boyfriend put her up to it."

At that, Sam and I exchanged a look. No one had mentioned Miriam finding a new partner after her husband died. If she was seeing someone, that would certainly explain why she was considering changing her will—and why her existing heir might want to stop her. It might also be why she planned to sell the house.

But why didn't Deborah or Barry tell us Miriam had started dating? It had been years since Liam Peabody died.

"We weren't aware that Miriam was seeing anyone," Sam said. He lowered his voice. "Was he married?"

"Oh, no, nothing like that." Gloria waved one hand as if to swat that sordid thought away. "We used to see them together everywhere. Worst kept secret in town."

"If she was a widow, and he's not married, why is it secret?" I asked.

"Oh, you know how it is. The state bar association doesn't like it when lawyers date their clients."

CHAPTER ELEVEN

Gloria's words stopped me in my tracks. When I'd talked to Barry yesterday, he'd seemed to have a soft spot for Miriam, but he never mentioned they'd been dating. Why would he keep it a secret? What else was he hiding?

"You're sure the two of them were a couple?" I asked.

"The whole town could tell he was sweet on her," she said. "It sure seemed like she returned the favor. There were even rumors that someone saw Barry in a jewelry store about a week before she died. Looking at diamond rings."

"He was planning to propose?" Sam said. "If Miriam got married, her will would change."

Everything fell into place. A change to the will could mean Deborah wouldn't inherit. Miriam's new husband—Barry, apparently—would be the heir. Giving Deborah a strong motive to kill her aunt before the wedding.

According to my vision, Miriam was planning to sell the house. Maybe she'd planned to move in with Barry. Did Deborah love that house enough to kill for it?

Abruptly, I grabbed the teapot off the counter. "Sam, let's go."

"Don't you want to wait to talk to a detective?" he asked.

"There's no time. Everything we've been doing is based on information from Barry. But if Barry lied about his relationship with Miriam, there's no telling what else he's been keeping from us."

Halfway to the car, I realized that Barry wouldn't be in his office on a Sunday morning, and we had no idea where he lived. I could call and ask him to meet us somewhere, but first, I went back into the police station.

There was no one like the town gossip to tell you where to find someone, and Gloria didn't disappoint. "Lunar Parish Church, over on Third Street. He goes to the nine o'clock mass."

Assuming mass lasted an hour, we had about fifteen minutes to get there before the service let out. And not much more than that before Deborah's flight left. She must be boarding. We were running out of time!

"Is it far?" My voice sounded desperate, even to my own ears.

"Nah. Head to the corner, turn right, go down two blocks. You can't miss it. It's the big white building with a million cars in front."

Right. I thanked her and left. She yelled behind me, asking me to come back with an update, but I pretended not to hear.

Sam and I made it to the church with a few minutes to spare, which was good because we had to park in the far corner of the lot. Gloria hadn't been kidding about the million cars.

"There's nothing like a romantic race through a parking lot on a beautiful Sunday morning," I said as we headed toward the massive double doors at the front of the building.

"Best first date I can imagine."

"Gee, I wish you'd told me about your low bar earlier. I wouldn't have made such exciting plans for this afternoon."

The wind took his response, and at that point, I couldn't maintain a conversation along with our current speed. When we made it to the steps outside the church, we skidded to a halt. Strains of a choir reached my ears, which probably meant we'd gotten here just in time. I'd barely managed to catch my breath from that mad dash when the right door opened, and an altar server came out. Two other servers followed, then the priest, then a ton of people.

All of a sudden, I wished I'd thought to stand back and survey the crowd from a distance. It could take forever to find Barry here.

Luckily, his loud wardrobe stood out. After a few minutes, Sam pointed to a hot-pink smoking jacket paired with lime-green plaid pants. "There he is!"

He chatted with an older couple as they all exited the doors. As soon as he saw us, Barry started patting his pockets in a now-familiar gesture. He stopped walking and turned to go back into the church. Then one of his companions touched his arm and held out a small metal object. He said something to her, then walked over to me and Sam while lighting a cigarette.

We moved out of the flow of people, trying to stay upwind.

"Good morning, Barry," Sam said.

"How can I help you?"

"Why didn't you tell us about your relationship with Miriam?" I asked.

His shoulders sagged. "I guess you've been talking to the town gossips. I knew you'd be here eventually."

"You lied to me," I said. "I trusted you. I've spent the last two days trying to help you."

"Aly deserves the truth," Sam said.

"We already know most of it," I added.

"We were childhood sweethearts," Barry said, not meeting my eyes. "She dumped me when she met Liam. Neither one of us came from money, you know. I did well over the years, going to law school and building a practice. But times were different then. Women didn't have as many options."

"She married Liam for his money?" That didn't make any sense. Barry wore suits that cost as much as my car. "But aren't you also rich?"

He laughed. "I do okay, but this all came from my practice. We were kids when she met Liam. She couldn't have known where my career would lead me."

How very sad for him. If Miriam had just been patient, the two of them could have had a nice life together.

"Why did you work for the family, if you had a history?" Sam asked.

"Liam never knew about our relationship," Barry said. "If I'd refused to work for him when I represented half the town, it would have been suspicious. Besides, I hadn't seen Miriam in ages at that point."

"And you fell in love again?" Sam asked.

"Oh, no," Barry said. "Not for a long time. We never had an affair, if that's what you think. I got married right after law school. I was always faithful to my wife."

While his words rang true, I'd have bet my psychic powers that Barry's love for Miriam never wavered. Something about his face when he talked about her spoke of true devotion. But how deep did that love go?

"Listen, Barry, if you loved Miriam, you have to help us. I know Deborah killed her, but I can't prove it."

He dabbed at the corners of his eyes with a handkerchief from his jacket pocket. "I know, I know. How can I help?"

"We need evidence. Can you think of anything at all that we might use? Was there cyanide in the house? The will gave Deborah motive, and her access to Miriam was opportunity, but we need more. Do you know any local doctors who might agree to re-examine the body?"

"Deborah had her cremated."

That information took all the wind out of my sails. Sam squeezed my hand for strength, but I didn't know what to say.

"Maybe we could talk to Geoff again?" Sam asked. "Do you know how we could contact him?"

"Sure, I've got his information right here." Barry pulled out his phone, and his face fell.

"What's wrong?"

The device blinked a red notification light. He turned it to face us. "Deborah's flight took off. She's gone."

CHAPTER TWELVE

The three of us stared at each other for a long time, trying to process the fact that we'd missed takeoff. All morning, I'd known time was tight, but I'd never given up the idea of finding evidence in time to stop Deborah.

It was too late. Deborah's plane left, and she was now in international air space. She got away with murder. Miriam would not be avenged, at least not by me. We'd failed.

"Can't we call Interpol and ask them to meet her flight when it lands?" Sam asked.

"The U.S. doesn't have an extradition treaty with Thailand." It was one of the many things I'd Googled when I couldn't sleep the night before. Searching for information beat tossing and turning and thinking about Sam lying on the other side of a thin wall. "That's probably why she chose it."

I hated failure, but I hated more being the only person in a position to help and not managing it. My eyes filled with tears.

"Hey. It's okay," Sam said, patting my hand.

"It's not okay. Miriam needed me."

"Getting Deborah arrested wouldn't bring Miriam back."

"I know, I get that." I sighed. "But I've got these powers, and that comes with some kind of responsibility, you know?"

To his credit, he didn't point out that I sounded like Spiderman.

"I know you feel that way. And I understand, really. But you can't blame yourself. If the universe wanted you to help, why not give you the power to coerce confessions? Or include a how-to manual so we know what you can do and how to do it? For that matter, the universe could send you visions before people died instead of after. That would be much more helpful."

"True." A weak smile crossed my lips. "Thanks."

"It's not entirely too late," Barry said. "The house isn't on the market yet. It's worth quite a bit, and if we can prove that Deborah killed Miriam, she won't get the money. That's the bulk of the estate."

"I guess that's something." I sighed. "I better call Rusty and let him know he doesn't need to keep looking for information on Deborah. Barry, you better hire a real private investigator. I clearly have no idea what I'm doing."

"This isn't your fault," Barry said. "Not a lot of people could crack a murder investigation in less than twenty-four hours. I have to go, but we'll talk later, okay?"

"Sure," I said dejectedly.

Sam took my hand and led me halfway across the parking lot before I remembered that I hadn't called Rusty yet. Normally, I'd text, but I wanted to make sure he knew to stop researching.

To my surprise, a gleeful cackle filled my ear when he answered.

"Hello?" I asked. "Are you okay?"

"Aly! Oh, this is awesome. Thanks for calling me yesterday. I'm laughing so hard, I'm crying."

"Yeah?" I put the phone on speaker so Sam could hear our conversation. "What am I missing? The tea set is a total dead end, and Deborah's plane took off a few minutes ago."

"Deborah's plane took off, sure. But she wasn't on it," Rusty said. "I called in an anonymous tip to TSA. They put her on the No-Fly List."

Was that even legal? I didn't know, and I didn't care. A ten-thousand-pound weight lifted off my shoulders as a peal of joyful laughter escaped me. "You're sure? She wasn't on the plane?"

"One thousand percent sure. Check her Twitter. She's pissed, but on her way back to New York City. The best part is, she doesn't even know why she was denied."

"Oh, Rusty! I could kiss you right now."

"Well, I'm not there and Sam is, so why don't you plant one on that gorgeous man instead?"

Not wanting to let down a friend, I complied. After about fifteen seconds, Rusty cleared his throat loudly into the speaker. "That's enough, guys."

We pulled apart, still grinning at each other like a couple of teenagers.

Sam asked, "What's the next step?"

"We need to confront Deborah with her motive and the murder weapon. And we need to do it before she finds another way out of the country." By the time I finished those three sentences, I'd nearly made it across the parking lot.

Sam trailed behind me. "I really think—"

"I know. But there's no time. Police are refusing to take us seriously, and we can't talk to anyone other than Gloria until tomorrow. We can't just sit around until then. You drive to Deborah's house while I look up New York law on recording a conversation."

He didn't argue, maybe realizing that I'd be going whether he helped me or not. Luckily, Rusty had given me Deborah's address along with Lindsay's. According to my good friend Google, New York allowed a person to record their own private conversation without fear of going to jail. Since I wasn't interested in committing a Class E felony, I was immensely relieved to hear it.

Sam and I planned while he drove, discussing all the buttons we could push to get Deborah to open up. Then I started Googling interrogation techniques. There had to be a way to crack this nut.

By the time we pulled up outside Deborah's building, I was about forty-five percent confident in my ability to get her to say something incriminating. Twelve percent confident that we'd find a parking space within about a mile of her home, and thirty-four percent confident it was about to rain.

"Do you want to just drop me off and circle the block?" I asked. "Maybe this won't take long."

"Sure! And then maybe we could drink some arsenic before we jump off the Brooklyn Bridge."

Before I could shoot back a biting response, a car's engine roared to life ahead of us. A familiar-looking man sat in the front seat, pulling on his seatbelt. In seconds, he adjusted his mirrors, signaled, and zoomed out in front of us.

"Is that Geoff?" Sam's voice echoed my thoughts.

"I think so, but do we go in or follow him?" I wasn't about to suggest we split up, because there was no time for the discussion that would spark.

"We're here to talk to Deborah. Let's go in."

As I crossed my fingers that we weren't making a mistake, he parked in the now-vacant space. The front door had a controlled entry system, so I pushed buttons until someone buzzed us in. Yay for people expecting food delivery. The building was a small walk-up, thankfully only three stories high. When we knocked on the door of Deborah's apartment, no one answered. Somehow, we hadn't considered the possibility that she wouldn't be home. I just assumed that after being denied a boarding pass, she'd come back here. Where else would she go?

The third time Sam banged for entry, the door swung open into an empty living area. The gold lock plate fell at the motion, swinging wildly from one screw.

"Deborah? Are you in there?" Sam called.

No answer.

We exchanged a look. In for a penny, in for a pound, right? Might as well take a look around. Maybe we'd find something interesting. A receipt for the plane ticket. The deed to a beach house in Thailand. Anything at all.

The apartment was small, an odd mess of tidiness and chaos. No dirty dishes in the sink. Drying rack empty, but cupboard doors open. Books strewn all over the living room. In the bedroom, we found the bed made. A peek in Deborah's tiny closet showed a lot of empty hangers, which was no surprise. No luggage anywhere, but clothes scattered on the floor. As if she'd cleaned before she left, but someone else had been here, searching.

Which also explained the door. Geoff had broken in.

"What do you think he was looking for?" Sam asked, as if reading my thoughts. Not the first time I'd wondered if he could do that.

"Maybe Geoff also suspects Deborah of killing Miriam. He could be looking for evidence."

My gaze continued to roam the apartment as we spoke. There had to be some clue here, something to tell us where Deborah would have gone. Finally, something on the ground caught my attention. A piece of paper on the floor, in most apartments, could have been there any amount of time, but given the juxtaposition of mess and tidiness, I suspected it had been dropped by whoever had done the search. I carefully picked the page up by the edges. A torn sheet, about three inches by four inches, of lined paper covered with handwriting. A research notebook?

I read the words aloud. "—ant showed up at the house today."

"Who?" Sam asked. "Ann?"

"No, it says 'ant,' but it's cut off. Lindsay Grant, maybe? No idea. They live nearby, so maybe. The next line says '—to pound sand. That's my—'."

"Hmm. Lindsay came to the house looking for Deborah or Geoff? Who wrote this?"

I shook my head. "I'm not sure. Deborah, I guess."

"Or Miriam. The paper looks old." Pulling out his phone, Sam snapped a picture of the page. A moment later, my phone beeped with a text. "Let's ask Deborah when we find her."

"Good plan."

"Do you want to go after Geoff before we go looking? He might know something."

"I think Deborah has to be our main priority," I said. "But where could she be? If I killed my aunt and my plans to leave the country got foiled, I feel like I'd still want some other way out of town."

"You think she's at Grand Central?"

"Maybe, but how on earth would we find her?" A sense of helplessness welled up in me. "We can't just call NYPD and tell them that a woman using a fake name is going to be passing through a major transportation hub on a busy weekend afternoon. What would we say? 'She's medium-height, with dark hair and dark eyes?'"

"When you put it like that..." He sighed. "Where could she have gone? It could take weeks to clear up the hold on her passport. I don't understand why she wouldn't come straight home to figure out her next step."

I'd been turning this over in my mind from the moment we saw the open door, because it was clear Deborah wouldn't be found inside. When I got stressed, I wanted to go places that calmed me down. The park where Kyle and I played after school on sunny days. The campus library. Mystic Pieces.

When I thought about it that way, the answer became immediately clear.

"Maybe she went to the museum," I said. "Her plans are unraveling. She could be upset. That's her happy place. She loves her job, remember?"

Sam was halfway down the stairs before I'd even finished explaining. The two of us got into his car without another word. While he called up the recent addresses on his GPS, I started looking for Deborah on social media. Nothing public since she apparently left the airport. I found one locked-down Facebook profile, with very little that I could view. Somehow, I doubted she would accept a friend request from me right now.

Before I figured out where else to look, we arrived at our destination. LaMonica was open to the public for free on Sundays, so no one sat at the entrance. That was both good and bad. We could have tried to convince an employee to take us to Deborah directly. But they also might have stalled us.

I skirted the lobby and went straight for the staircase. "Sam, stay here and watch the elevators."

"You know that's not going to happen."

"I don't have time to argue!" One look at his face made me feel bad. He was only trying to keep me safe. "How about this? Wait here until I get to the top of the stairs. I promise to text you when it's safe to come up. I just don't want her to leave one way while we go in the other."

"Isn't there a back staircase?"

Oh, no. He was right. Also, this was a terrible plan. We'd never find Deborah by going to every place she liked in New York City. What was next? Central Park, FAO Schwartz, the Empire State Building?

Sam must have seen the realization dawn on my face, because he stopped arguing. "I'm on it. Scream if you see her."

With that, he turned and bolted across the open floor plan, deftly dodging three glass exhibit cases before pelting through the open doorway leading to the back. Turning toward the stairs, I did the same.

At the fourth-floor landing, I paused to get my bearings. When Deborah gave us the tour, we'd come up in the elevator. A sign on the wall pointed me at the DaVinci room on the right, the Greek room on the left, and the pi room ahead of me. No offices. Beside the elevator sat the restrooms. The offices would probably be far away from the most heavily trafficked areas, plus Sam hadn't come up through the back yet, so I went straight through the doorway.

A-ha! Halfway across the back room, a door sat closed in the wall. A familiar sign on the door said *Private. Do Not Enter.*

Across the room, Sam appeared at the top of the staircase. He spotted the door at the same time I did. He caught my eyes and pointed. I nodded silently, and we crept toward it. Now that we were between Deborah and the exits, stealth mattered more than speed. We wanted the element of surprise.

He reached for the knob and turned. Thankfully, it was unlocked. Twenty feet inside sat another door: this one with an electronic keypad.

Sam stopped. "Any idea how to get through the door?"

"Let's set off the fire alarm and wait for her to come out."

His eyes widened. "Aly!"

I giggled. "Kidding. Give me a sec. Your mom and I were trying something yesterday."

The keypad was a grid of twelve blank squares. You must need to touch it to turn it on. Reaching out, I held my hand in front of the device. Nothing happened. No big surprise. Okay then. I poked the bottom button. The device whirred. Suddenly, *Start* appeared in the key in the lower-left corner and *Reset* in the lower right. Numbers, zero through nine, filled in the remaining keys like on a telephone keypad.

"Any ideas what the code might be?" Sam asked.

"Just one."

Maybe practice was all it would take to hone this particular skill. Or maybe it would only work when I'd met the person, or if they'd been in a state of high anxiety while inputting their code. I didn't know, but Olive's experiment had piqued my interest, and I wanted to try again.

Taking a deep breath, I reached for the *Reset* button and focused on Deborah. Sam vanished as soon as I pressed it.

A well-manicured hand reached out, pressing Start. The machinery whirred, and ten digits appeared on the keys, but not in numerical order. They popped up randomly. The hand paused as I studied the red numerals. Then the fingers reached out and punched in 1-7-45.

Miriam's birthday? How sweet. Or weirdly morbid.

I coughed, bringing me back to myself. Then I punched in the code. The keypad beeped. A light over the door turned green, and the deadbolt clacked open.

"Wow. Good job." Sam grabbed the handle and swung the door open. "After you."

Having never been in the offices before, I didn't quite know what to expect. We found ourselves in a hallway with three doors. A plaque on the door in the middle of the right wall said *Curator*.

A police officer stood outside the door, his back to the wall, as if guarding it. Maybe they'd come to arrest her! A huge smile split my face in two. Now everything would be okay. Deborah would be taken to jail, and Sam and I could go explore Kevin's storage unit like we originally planned. I'd be back in Shady Grove, snuggling with Kyle by bedtime. After only a day away, I missed that little face.

Sam's voice cut through my thoughts. "Is everything okay, Officer?"

It wasn't until I heard his tone that I realized maybe this wasn't the time for celebration, as I thought. Peeking through the cracked door, I saw another officer inside the room, pacing and talking into his phone. I couldn't make out the words.

"No, son, I'm afraid everything is not okay," the officer said. "How do you know Ms. Peabody?"

"We met her at an estate sale yesterday," Sam said. "She

promised to show us around the museum last night, but she got distracted so we came back to see if she was free now."

His quick thinking made me want to kiss him.

The officer's face softened. "Well, I'm afraid you're not going to get that tour."

"Is Deborah going to jail?" I asked.

"I'm afraid not, miss."

Oh, man. She couldn't get away, not after all this. "Listen, I know this is going to sound crazy, but you need to arrest her. Deborah Peabody killed her aunt."

"We can't arrest her. She's dead."

CHAPTER THIRTEEN

With one hand over my mouth, I staggered backward and slumped against the wall. My brain couldn't quite process the officer's words. Deborah was dead. How? Why?

"Are you sure?" I asked.

"Affirmative. We've been doing this a long time," the officer said.

Now I understood why the other officer was talking into his phone and not speaking to Deborah or handcuffing her. He must be calling an ambulance to come and take her away. I moved toward the doorway, but he stepped in front of me.

"I can't let you go in there. It's a crime scene."

"I can help! Call the Shady Grove police. I've helped them solve two crimes."

Sam stepped forward, drawing the officer's attention away from me. "Deborah just inherited a lot of money. Do you think she was murdered?"

"Unlikely, son. She left a suicide note."

Why would Deborah kill herself when she was only hours away from escape? The Canadian border wasn't that far. She could have rented a car at the airport, headed north, and been enjoying poutine for her dinner. None of this made sense. I needed to see the note. There had to be a way inside the room.

As if someone was looking out for me, the officer's phone rang. He glanced at the screen, then pointed toward the door. "I have to take this. We've got this under control. You should go."

Before we could respond, he took the call and disappeared through the door to Deborah's office. I couldn't see where he went or the other officer, but I needed to go inside.

Two steps from the door, Sam caught my arm. "Please don't get arrested."

"I have to see what happened. I might get a vision!"

"I know, but..." He sighed and ran his fingers through his hair. "At least let me distract them for you."

Right. Good point. I nodded and flattened myself against the wall. Sam walked back toward the exit, then dropped to his knees, screaming. "Oh, this is terrible! I feel faint. I can't breathe! Somebody help me!"

His performance seemed exaggerated to me, but all it had to do was cause a commotion. He certainly did that. The door to Deborah's office swung outward, and Officer #2 appeared. Without even glancing at me, he raced to Sam's side. I snuck past him, through the opening. Deborah's desk was against the far wall. She sat there, slumped forward. Since nothing could be gained from touching her, I looked at the desk to see what I could find.

A mostly full teacup, steam still rising from the top. The lipstick on the rim matched the shade Deborah had worn yesterday. Beside it, I spotted what I was looking for.

A piece of paper with a large monogrammed *P* at the top.

It's over. I'm sorry.

That was all it said. Sam was right, Deborah must've realized we were onto her. If we tested the tea in her cup, I suspected it would contain the same poison she'd used to murder her aunt. That was a police matter, though. My powers didn't extend to detecting toxic substances.

"Hey! You can't be in here!"

Uh-oh. Officer #1 was back. "Sorry, I was uh, looking for the bathroom."

"If you don't leave right now, I'll have you arrested for desecrating a crime scene. We've had too many problems with you kids posting photos on Instagram. Not everything needs to be public."

He continued his lecture all the way to the door until I found myself deposited outside the keypad where Sam now stood, looking sheepish. We walked silently toward the stairs.

When the door closed behind us, he asked, "Did you see anything?"

"I saw her. She's..." I swallowed. "And the note. I don't know why or how, but she's gone."

Outside, we called Barry to relay the news. He took the news well, all things considered. After a few minutes, I hung up. Something still didn't sit right with all this. The case felt unfinished. Like I hadn't done enough to fix everything.

Beside me, Sam said, "I'm sorry. I know how badly you wanted to bring her to justice."

"It's okay." I swallowed back a lump in my throat. "Miriam can be at peace now."

Deborah's death left me drained. After the stress of the past twenty-four hours, only to have everything end so abruptly, I wanted to sleep for a year. But I wasn't ready to head back to Shady Grove yet. I'd had two purposes for coming to the city, and the second had been delayed long enough.

After all this time, when Sam parked in the lot behind Joey's Storage, I couldn't quite believe we'd made it. I'd found the key to Kevin's secret storage unit hidden in the depths of a box full of cords in our basement weeks ago. After months of scouring our house for anything that belonged to Katrina, any object where I might finally get a reading, I'd been ecstatic to find the key. Then I'd realized that the unit remained in the suburb where Kevin and Katrina lived before she died, two hours from home.

I'd tried to get here right away, using my budding relationship with Sam as an excuse. Unfortunately, Kyle came down with a fever that morning, and the trip got canceled. Anyway, here I was, finally!

With my very own copy of Kevin's swiped key. Not that

I expected him to go looking for the original all of a sudden, but I liked to have my bases covered.

The building advertised more than a hundred temperature-controlled units, twenty-four-hour security, and electronic access. Luckily, Kevin never locked his laptop at home, so it was pretty easy for me to access his saved passwords on his computer while he was in the shower. I had five possibilities to try.

The third time I entered a code into the keypad, the door swung open. I let out a squeal of delight.

Sam and I strode confidently down the hallway, keeping our faces averted from the cameras I'd spent significant time scouting in any images I could find of the building online. I couldn't imagine Kevin showing up and demanding to watch the footage, but stranger things had happened.

Looking around at the blindingly bright overhead lights and the vibrant carpet designed to hide stains rather than enhance anything, Sam said, "You know, I always wanted my first date with a beautiful woman to be committing a misdemeanor."

"Technically, our first date was that race across the parking lot," I said. Then the first part of his sentence sank in. "Beautiful?"

"Yeah. I've been waiting for a date for a long time."

"Me, too. I was hoping for something a little more low-key than breaking and entering though."

"I tried that," he said. "We had that amazing kiss and then you ditched me to solve a murder, so we never got our dinner."

"I thought that was an apology dinner, not a date."

"That was a date framed as an apology so my fragile ego didn't have to risk rejection."

I turned to face him. Our fingers entwined in that way

where you're not really sure who reached for whom first. Gazing into his eyes, I raised up enough to kiss him lightly, then dropped back down. "In the entire time we've known each other, there was never a single second I would've said no to dinner with you."

He grinned, one of those smiles that made his whole face glow. "Same."

"Now let's finish the law-breaking. There are more smooches where that came from."

He bowed dramatically. "After you."

Up the stairs, down the hall, we strode purposefully to unit number seventy-four. From the outside, it looked like all the others. For some reason, I expected it to glow or have a pointing arrow or something.

"This feels anti-climactic," Sam said.

I smiled at the way he echoed my thoughts. "Feels silly, right? It's just a unit, but what else would it be? Ah, well. Let's go in."

When the key slid into the lock, I held my breath. After all this time, if we'd turned out to be in the wrong place, or if the key had been to some old, long-closed unit, I might have cried. It turned easily, and the lock clacked open.

Sam squeezed my hand, letting me know he understood my stress. Together, we pulled the door open and went inside.

A huge sigh of relief whooshed out of me as a sea of boxes and the unmistakable fragrance of vanilla hit my nose. Until that moment, I'd nearly forgotten Katrina's signature scent. At the funeral, there were vanilla candles everywhere. Wardrobe boxes stood in the corner, including a giant box that had to hold her wedding dress. My gaze went right to it.

I shouldn't.

So many of Katrina's things sat in this space. I didn't need to go instantly to the most important one. Even though Katrina would never have a daughter, it wasn't for me to decide what to do with that dress.

"Where do you want to start?" Sam asked.

"In theory, one day, my powers will reach the point where I can touch almost anything and get a vision if I want to summon one," I said. "But I'm not there yet. Let's see what's in each box and go from there."

Kevin had meticulously labeled the containers before he brought them here. Not only did bold, black marker declare which room each box was from, but he'd also taped a list of the contents to the side of every single one. After a moment's exploration, I discovered he'd also color-coded the tape on the boxes. Red for clothes, blue for toiletries, silver for jewelry.

"Here." As soon as I spotted the last, I ripped it open eagerly.

Necklaces, bracelets, earrings, an anklet. Her hospital bracelet from when Kyle was born. One at a time, I put each piece on, hoping and praying to trigger some kind of response. When I picked up a necklace, I closed my eyes and pictured Katrina standing at the bathroom mirror, doing the same.

Unfortunately, I'd never seen the master bathroom at the old house, and Katrina never set foot in the one we had now. I didn't know if that made a difference, but none of the stuff in her jewelry box gave me any information.

"What about her wedding rings?" Sam asked.

I swept my fingers through the box again, sifting each item through my fingers. "It's not here. Either Kev kept them for Kyle, or she was buried with them."

"I'm sorry, Aly." He kissed me softly. "I'm sure we'll find something."

"Yeah. Let's keep going."

Turned out, Katrina owned a lot of stuff. I tried on oven mitts, pretended to apply old makeup, pulled one maternity shirt after another over my head. A couple of them gave me hints: flashes of happiness, of joyful anticipation. Seeing how excited Katrina must've been to give birth made me both happy and sad. She'd never get to see her little boy grow up. She never watched him count the stairs as he walked up, saying "ebeben" each time he got to the eleventh one or sat beside the bathtub while he gleefully splashed her declaring, "Water is wet!"

Blinking back tears, I moved on, going through one box after another while Sam followed in my wake, repacking and trying to make it appear we'd never been here. Everything looked pretty good, but I'd have to come back with multicolored rolls of packing tape next time I was in town.

Finally, after two hours, the second-to-last box was opened, sifted through, and told me nothing. Sam had repacked Katrina's belongings carefully. Not a single item had given me any useful hint of Katrina or her death. I was starting to doubt whether I actually had powers after all. Maybe the last few months had been a waking dream.

With a heavy sigh, I allowed my gaze to return at long last to the wedding dress box against the far wall. "I can't."

"Are you sure?" Sam asked.

"What's the point? Not a single object in here has told me anything."

"You're going to give up without trying the last one? Without using the item that will show you the happiest day of your sister-in-law's life."

In reply, I sank onto the nearest box and buried my

head in my hands. "But why that particular item? Why, of every single thing in here, can I get nothing off of anything less personal? I don't get it."

"I know. I'm sorry. I don't get how this works."

"Me, neither." I sighed. "I saw Katrina's death."

"What? Just now? Why didn't you say anything?"

"No, not just now. When I was trying to find Professor Zimm's murderer."

"The same person killed Professor Zimm and your sister-in-law?" Sam looked understandably confused, considering that Katrina died more than a year earlier and about a hundred miles away from my former teacher.

"No, sorry." I explained how I'd found an old mirror from the McMansion under Kevin's bed, and I'd been teaching myself to scry in it after my efforts to induce a regular vision failed. "And eventually, I saw it. She argued with someone I didn't recognize about Kyle."

"Someone she knew?"

"Yeah. I couldn't see enough to tell who it was, but their conversation made it seem like they knew each other."

"Okay, good. That helps," he said.

"A little. Whoever it was discovered a strong psychic presence in their house and went looking for it. Katrina pretended that she was the one with powers, that they wanted her. I don't know if she knew it was Kyle or thought she was protecting Kevin. Then she attacked them, and— she lost the fight."

I blinked back tears at the memory. Sam cupped my face and kissed my tears away before resting his forehead against mine. I sank into him, accepting both the comfort and the strength he offered.

"You don't have any idea who the killer was?" he asked.

"No clue," I admitted. "Thin. Pale skin. A tattoo that

might have been barbed wire or ivy on one wrist. That's it. Whoever it was wore a hood. I couldn't see a face, couldn't even tell a gender."

"Do you think you'd recognize it if you saw it again?"

"The black hoodie? Doubtful."

"The tattoo," Sam said.

"Oh." I shrugged. "Honestly, I don't know. I only caught a glimpse. That's why I was hoping to find something here that would either give me...I don't even know. Something helpful."

"Maybe we could try visiting some local tattoo artists to look at pictures of their work," he said. "It's worth a shot."

"That's a great idea. Thanks." I took a deep breath. "Enough stalling. Time to try on the dress."

My chest tightened as Sam brought the box to me. He knew how hard it would be for me to even walk across the room to open it. Together, we slit the tape and pulled open the lid, raising the flaps one at a time. First, I removed a wide, flat box marked *veil*. Sam lifted a smaller square box out and set it carefully aside. Nothing left but the dress. Since Sam was several inches taller than me (as was Katrina), I gestured for him to lift it out. Doing it myself would mean toppling over backward and smothering myself with the dress when I tried to clear the bottom of the train from the cardboard container.

Katrina and I weren't close to the same size, so I had to improvise. We unzipped the dress, and Sam helped me step in. I didn't bother to ask him to zip it. It was at least a foot too long, not counting the train. Instead, he held out the front and I slipped my arms through the spaghetti straps, hooking them over my elbows.

"You look beautiful," Sam said with mischief in his eyes.

"Hush," I said. "I'm concentrating. Hand me the veil?"

"Sure, hold on." He went back to the box. "Do you want the bouquet, too?"

"Her bouquet is in the box? How?"

"It's been dried and preserved."

"Thanks, but no." I was doing enough harm to Katrina's most treasured possessions. I didn't need to literally crumble her wedding flowers into dust.

Sam handed me the veil, which I settled onto my head as best I could. Then I pulled the filmy layer over my face, took a deep breath, and clasped my hands in front of my chest. I prayed this worked because I'd topple if Sam tried to walk me down the aisle.

The slab walls of the storage unit shimmered out of sight, replaced by the Gothic architecture of the church Kevin and Katrina never attended except on their wedding day. And her funeral. I swallowed my sadness, forcing myself to focus on the vision.

Sam no longer stood in front of me. *I peered through a set of open double doors. Rows of wooden pews stretched on either side of an aisle carpeted in red velvet and peppered with white rose petals. A woman in a blue dress walked further ahead. Seeing distance in a vision wasn't typically as good as real life, so I couldn't tell much about her. Her pace and the placement said "bridesmaid." She moved beyond the edges of my sight. The unmistakable opening strains of "Here Comes the Bride" played. Hundreds of people rose from the pews. They all turned to look at me.*

"You ready?"

Until he spoke, I hadn't realized a man stood beside me in the vision. Knowing Katrina's father hadn't been around much, I had no idea who he was. Mary's father, maybe? The families clearly spent a lot of time together. Whoever he was, Katrina knew him well.

A smile spread across my face. "You know I am. I've been waiting for this day my whole life."

We walked through the church doors side-by-side. Every eye in the place was on me. I looked from the man I loved, waiting beside the priest at the altar, to all the friends and family who had come to share this day with us. With a jolt, I realized I looked into my own, much younger face. So weird. I'd never appeared in my own vision before. *Then my gaze shifted back to Kevin, and I stood at the front.*

I held out my bouquet to hand it off to my bridesmaid, still looking at Kevin. An arm snaked across my peripheral vision to take the flowers. Sunlight filtering in through the windows caught her sapphire bracelet, presumably chosen to match the dress. It circled her wrist, but it wasn't the only thing. Beneath the metal, the woman wore a tattoo of a rose-bud. Blood red, with a green vine trailing up toward her elbow. A couple of leaves.

I'd seen that vine before.

In another vision.

CHAPTER FIFTEEN

For a long moment, I couldn't tear my eyes away from the tattoo on the woman's arm. The image that was so familiar, yet it belonged to a person I didn't know. The same one I'd seen in the mirror. It wasn't wire or ivy. It was a vine. *Stifling a gasp, I raised my gaze to look into the woman's face. She was gone.*

The church evaporated, and I once again stood beside Sam in a temperature-controlled storage unit, surrounded by my dead sister-in-law's belongings.

"Aly? Are you okay?"

I couldn't breathe. Could barely see. I needed out of Katrina's dress, away from all of this. "Get it off!"

Sam moved instantly, pulling the dress straps down and away from me even as I ripped the veil from my head and dropped onto the lid of the nearest box.

"What happened?"

Tears streamed down my cheeks. "It was their wedding. Such a happy day. I remember it—I even saw myself in the church."

"Nothing about the murderer? I'm sorry, Al."

No one else called me Al. The shortened version of my nickname made me smile. I took a deep breath. "No, I saw the murderer. It was Katrina's Maid of Honor."

Sam repeated my words. "Katrina's Maid of Honor killed her. Are you sure?"

"Pretty sure. I mean, not anything admissible in court, but yeah, I think so." He listened with wide eyes while I recounted the details of my vision. "I didn't see her face, but whoever took Katrina's bouquet from her when she got to the front of the church has the same tattoo. That's the Maid of Honor's job."

"Who was it? You were at the wedding, weren't you?"

Since Kevin was nine years older than me, I'd been in high school when he married. He'd moved to New York City for college and only brought Katrina home to visit once or twice before the wedding. She'd seemed nice enough, but we didn't exactly spend all our time together talking about her closest friends.

"Yeah, but I didn't know anyone. The main thing I remember was my cousin's son hitting on me. It was weird."

Sam took a deep breath. "Don't get mad—"

"You know that phrase has never once gotten the desired result, right?"

"But you didn't see a face in your visions, and you don't remember anything from the wedding. You only saw parts of a tattoo. You don't know who they belong to. It wasn't necessarily the Maid of Honor who took her bouquet. It could have been any bridesmaid."

Some people would have been irritated but... well, okay, I was a little irritated. One of the things I liked about Sam was that he helped keep me grounded. More than once, I wondered if he had some empathic abilities. But right now, I wanted to rush off and accuse someone of murder. After the last twenty-four hours, almost anyone would do.

Really, Sam was keeping me from getting sued and possibly thrown in jail. On that note, I bit back a sarcastic remark. "I'm not mad. I don't love that you're right, but I'm not mad at you. Also—I've met two people in the last two months who I thought were Mary. Either of them could be the killer. For that matter, they could be the same person."

"Right. And that person may or may not be actually her."

"I'm getting dizzy," I said. "This is all too much."

"Have you had any luck getting back into Destiny's Haven?" Sam asked.

"Not yet. But maybe something here will give me an idea of what to ask when I get back in there."

"Makes sense." He moved around me, folding the dress and repacking it into the box. I helped in silence. After the lid was closed and taped again, he spoke. "I have an idea."

"Awesome."

"Not about Mary, not specifically. It's stifling in here. We're surrounded by Katrina's stuff. We've been running around for hours, and we haven't eaten since breakfast. Let's grab her wedding album, plus the DVD, and get out of here."

"You don't have a DVD player." We'd had a long talk once about how he believed streaming was superior in every way, until I'd pointed out that sometimes the internet stops working.

He sighed. "You're right, but Mom does. So do you and Kevin. We'll look through the album to confirm which member of the wedding party has the tattoo. You can watch the video after you get back to Shady Grove. Then we'll figure out how to locate that person or see if we can find out where the tattoo is done. Some of these places do real art, and they display it proudly. The artist would probably happily take credit."

"You mentioned that earlier. What are the odds it was done somewhere in New York City?"

"Considering you said Katrina and Kevin met at Columbia and held the wedding nearby? It's certainly possible. But New York has a lot of tattoo parlors. I wouldn't get my hopes up." He moved boxes around as he spoke, searching for the albums.

"You're right. That's not a project for today, anyway. I have to get home because I'm on Kyle duty tomorrow. I'll make a list of places on the train ride." I sighed. "Let's go."

Since we'd already gone through everything once, we were back in the car a few minutes later. Part of me wanted to rip the top album open and dive in, but my growling stomach convinced me to wait. Hungry Aly would impatiently flip the pages, then drip greasy pizza everywhere while she tried to multitask in a moving vehicle.

Instead, Sam pulled into the lot of a small fast-food place on the way back to the highway. They had a drive-thru, but we were a good half hour from Sam's apartment if the traffic gods were in our favor. Cold French fries were no one's friend. We carried the albums with us while I tried to mentally calculate the likelihood that anyone eating at Disco Burger would have brought a portable DVD player with them, and that they'd let two random strangers borrow it.

Once we ordered, Sam waited for our food while I filled our drinks and found a corner booth so we could sit side-by-side to look at the pictures.

The first album must've weighed about fifteen pounds, and I placed it reverently on the table, as far as possible from our iced beverages. These albums weren't mine to ruin, and I'd never forgive myself if a bit of fast-food condensation messed up Kevin's treasured memories. Kyle would look through these someday.

My heart fluttered with excitement. I was on the verge of something here, I knew it.

Gold was element number seventy-nine, atomic symbol Au. A precious metal, which was why it was used in this stuff. Element eighty was mercury, which was less romantic and more deadly.

As I reviewed the elements, I traced the embossed gold letters on the front with one finger. *OUR WEDDING.* Inside this album, pictures of the wedding party would reveal the person wearing a tattoo of rose vines. Mom might remember who the other members of the wedding party were, but if not, well—Kevin never locked his computer, and he had Facebook. Surely, I'd be able to track down some of them once I got home.

Sam placed a tray on the table and slid into the booth beside me. "Are you going to look at the pictures or just admire the cover all day?"

The glorious scent of deep-fried potatoes reached my nose, and my stomach howled in response. "Just look for now. I need to eat."

"Here." He picked up a fry and held it to my lips. "Go ahead and take a peek. I'll handle the fries."

"You are by far the best person in the world."

"Am I? Or is this all part of my devious plan to ensure I get more fries?"

I snorted at him, took a big bite, and opened the book. A program taped inside the front cover reminded me of the date of the ceremony, the location, and the names of the entire wedding party. Bingo.

Maid of Honor: Mary Towne. No surprise there. Katrina's sister, and my number one suspect. Sort of.

"Priscilla Towne," Sam read over my shoulder. "Did Katrina have more than one sister?"

The remaining bridesmaids were listed alphabetically, so it took me a second to find what he was referring to. There she was, at the end of the list. "Not that I know of. Maybe there was a secret twin?"

"It sounds like you've been watching too many soap operas again."

"I can't help it! *As the Hospital Guides Our Lives* has every episode online, and it's great background noise for studying." When I realized he was just giving me a hard time, I returned to the subject in front of us. "Okay, not a secret twin."

"I believe *secret* twins also aren't usually in a person's wedding party," Sam pointed out. "A cousin, maybe?"

"Or, it could be magic. We already know Mary's a witch."

The remaining names on the program meant nothing to me, so I turned the page after Sam gave me a sip of soda. I skipped past the formal engagement photo: lovely, but not informative. When "Mary" met with me to give me that cursed rocking horse, I'd pored over her photo albums, trying desperately to get one of the photographs to spark a vision. It hadn't worked, so I focused on finding information the old-fashioned way: with my eyeballs. The next several pages included pictures of Kevin and his groomsmen, getting ready for the big event. Seeing my brother looking so young and carefree brought a pang to my heart. These days, he seemed so weighted-down. I needed to resolve this for his sake.

On the next page, I spotted what I was looking for:

several carefully staged shots of the bridal party getting ready for the big day, designed to look spontaneous. Katrina in a bathrobe with curlers in her hair. Mary applying mascara, mouth opened comically wider than necessary. Three women I didn't know in varying states of readiness.

"Who's that?" Sam nodded toward the page with a French fry, not touching it. Leaning forward, I nipped it out of his hand. "She looks a lot like the pictures of your sister-in-law."

"Probably Mary. Are you talking about the brunette with the bob?" My finger hovered above one of the pictures.

"Nope. Look at the redhead."

It took me a minute to find a picture of the woman's face. Lots of makeup, brown eyes hidden behind glasses, heart-shaped lips. Lovely, but a stranger. I shook my head. "Must be one of the bridesmaids. Why?"

"Because she looks a lot like Katrina." Taking three napkins, Sam folded them and wrapped one so it covered the redhead's hair, leaving only her features. Then he did the same with Mary and Katrina.

"Whoa. They could be sisters."

"Are you sure they're not?"

I nodded. "Positive. Katrina only had one sister. But that could be another relative. What was that other name?"

"Priscilla, right?" Sam already had his phone in hand. "On it."

The longer I stared at the picture, the more clearly I saw the woman's face. She had features extremely similar to the person I'd met recently, who claimed to be Katrina's sister Mary. Equally similar to the woman currently staying under Mary's name at Destiny's Haven, who claimed not to be her.

Katrina never knew her father. If she grew up with

cousins, it would have been one of her mother's relatives. As the realization hit me, I slammed my fist down on the table. Ow.

"What's wrong?" Sam asked.

The DNA test I'd run said that the sample I'd used came from someone with the same mitochondrial DNA as Kyle. That meant they shared a female ancestor, so I'd assumed it was Mary.

Was Priscilla the person who contacted me? And if so, why was she pretending to be someone else? Or was Priscilla the person locked up in Destiny's Haven?

"This changes everything," I said. "After running the DNA test, I was operating under the assumption that the woman at Destiny's Haven lied, that she was Mary after all."

"But it might be someone else."

"Cousins have a common grandparent. If Mary and Priscilla share a grandmother, they also share the same mitochondrial DNA."

He got it instantly. "As would Kyle."

"Yup."

"It's okay. We'll keep looking."

For ten minutes, I fumed while eating the rest of my lunch and letting Sam search for information about Priscilla on his phone. Childish, yes, but what a frustrating setback. Finally, I asked, "Find anything?"

"Priscilla has a Facebook page, but it's not terribly informative," Sam said. "She's got almost two thousand friends. Either she's not married, or her relationship status isn't public. She really likes *The Real Housewives* shows. All of them. I'll dig into it more once I get home."

"Thanks. Speaking of home, let's find a close-up of the tattoo so we can get out of here."

I skimmed the pages, looking for any images that would help. The wedding photographer unfortunately hadn't been terribly interested in preserving the wrists of the bridal party. We went past at least a dozen images before my breath caught in my throat. I stopped and stared.

"Did you find it?"

Wordlessly, I pointed at the picture.

Sam's mouth dropped open. There it was. A gorgeously detailed rose with a vine trailing away. Two leaves on the vine, one shaped like a K. The others represented four different letters: M. C. P. N. Five women in the photo, each sporting a nearly identical tattoo.

CHAPTER SIXTEEN

Argh! Four different women had that same tattoo, not counting Katrina. All of a sudden, I doubted everything I thought I knew. Maybe it had been Katrina's wrist I saw in the vision, not the killer's. In that case, looking for the tattoo would be a colossal waste of time. Just when it seemed like I was making progress, another setback hit.

Sam squeezed my hand. "Hey. I know this feels frustrating, but you're making huge progress. You've narrowed your suspect list from every single person in the world to the members of the bridal party."

I offered him a small smile. "When you put it like that, it doesn't seem so bad. But what if I saw Katrina's tattoo when I scryed the mirror, not the killer's?"

"Close your eyes," he said.

I obeyed.

"Can you call up the image in your mind?"

It took a long moment of reciting the elements of the periodic table to calm myself enough to answer that question. Around the time I got to element twenty-two, titanium, I felt sort of human. The image came to me. "Got it."

"Tell me what you see."

"The tattoo is peeking out of the sleeve of a dark-colored shirt. Katrina's wearing a lilac V-neck t-shirt."

"It's not her arm, then."

I shook my head. "No. She's got short sleeves, and the killer is wearing long sleeves. I don't see a tattoo on Katrina's arm."

"Do you know where Katrina's tattoo was?"

"No idea. I never saw it when she was alive. I'll look through more albums later." As usual, having a plan lifted my spirits, even if it was as half-formed as "look at photo albums." I could also ask Kevin if I could think of some way to do it without raising his suspicions.

"Great!" Sam said. "Meanwhile, this is good news. We know Katrina didn't kill herself, so that gives you four suspects. What can you tell me about them?"

Very little, actually.

"Well, whoever this woman is, she's not the killer." I pointed at an Eastern-Asian-looking woman standing to Katrina's right. "The person in my vision was definitely white, and the tattoo wasn't on their shoulder."

"Great! See? One down already."

I gave him a wry smile. "Thanks."

On Katrina's other side stood Mary and the woman who had to be Priscilla. They stood with their arms around each other, beaming at the camera with matching smiles on their nearly identical faces.

I couldn't swear if I'd met either or both of them. Even if the images showed one of them was Maid of Honor—as I suspected it would—that wouldn't necessarily help me.

"I know this is frustrating," Sam said. "But you really are making progress. We know that you met Mary and/or

Priscilla and one of them most likely killed Katrina. That's huge."

"You're right. It is huge. I just wish I didn't have so many unanswered questions."

TEN MINUTES LATER, we were back in the car. Although it had been a long and exhausting weekend, we had one more thing to do. Before I headed back to Shady Grove, Sam took me to visit Christie Perez, one of Katrina's bridesmaids who, unlike Pricilla, laid her whole life out on Facebook for everyone to see. She featured prominently in the photo album, and she had a tattoo like the one in the picture. Based on the images, she appeared to be shorter than Katrina, but so were all the bridesmaids except Naomi. We needed to talk to Christie, see if she had a motive, find out what she was doing the day her friend was killed.

Alternatively, if she would show us a tattoo of rose vines anywhere other than on her wrist, we could at least cross her name off the suspect list.

According to her online profile, Christie managed a small bakery in New Jersey, focusing on wedding cakes. As much as I longed to pretend Sam and I were getting married, ask to taste a dozen yummy cakes while squeezing his hand and gazing longingly into his eyes, that was a great way to get distracted fast. Instead, I told her that I was making a memory book of Katrina for Kyle so he'd have something of his mother.

A nice idea, actually. I should get on that.

Although she wore a white chef's coat instead of a ball gown and her hair was scraped back into a bun, we recognized Christie instantly from the photo album. Same wide-set eyes behind large round glasses. Same friendly smile and crooked bottom teeth, less makeup. She greeted us warmly.

"How well did you know Katrina?" I asked after we introduced ourselves.

"She was my best friend," Christie said, blinking several times. "We met a million years ago, back when we were at Ross School. Sat through the same honors classes, applied to Columbia together. Sometimes, I still pick up the phone to text her. I can't believe she's gone."

"I didn't realize you'd gone to the same college," I said.

"We didn't. I'd realized by then that academia wasn't my thing, so I went to culinary school instead. Best decision I ever made. But Katrina loved the Ivy League, loved learning. I introduced her to Kevin. Did you know that?"

I sat up straighter, leaned forward. "You did? I thought they met at Columbia."

"They did, but only because I was there every week, visiting Katrina. At one point, I started dating this guy who turned out to be Kevin's roommate. Nice guy, cute, but duller than a box of rocks. I realized early on that while Trevor wasn't going to be my happily ever after, his roommate was exactly the kind of nerd Katrina would love. And I was right."

Sam leaned forward. "Christie, if you and Katrina were best friends since you were kids, does that mean you were also friends with Mary?"

"Sure," she said. "The four of us hung out all the time."

"Hold on," I said. "The four of you?"

"Sure. Me, Kat, Mary, and their cousin, Prissy."

Priscilla. The fifth name in the program. The woman who looked quite a bit like Mary and Katrina. All the evidence suggested I'd met her recently, although I still didn't know if she was the woman claiming to be Mary or the one insisting she wasn't.

Sam put it together faster than I did. "You were so close, you got matching tattoos."

Christie laughed. "We did! Mine is on my lower back, so I tend to forget about it until I walk by the mirror after a shower. But you're right, it's there. How did you know?"

"We were looking at the wedding album the other day," I said. "Saw the image with all the tattoos, but we didn't know who had which one."

"Katrina and I went with the tramp stamp," she said. "We liked to do everything together, but I think she also wanted to be able to hide hers, even in a bathing suit."

"What about the others?"

"Naomi got hers on the back of her shoulder. She was Katrina's roommate the first two years at Columbia."

Naomi Yamamoto had never been on my suspect list, since Katrina's killer had pale white skin and was shorter than Katrina. Still, it might help to talk to her. She had been around; she must have interacted with everyone.

"How well did you know Naomi?"

"Extremely well. Since she was Katrina's roommate, I saw her all the time. She was big in drama, always busy learning lines or studying or something. Sometimes we read with her, that was fun."

"That's so cool!" Interviewing an actress seemed more difficult than your average person, but she might know something about Katrina's other friends. I tried to play it cool. "I'd love to talk to her. Did she stay in the city to act?"

"Oh, no." Christie shook her head. "Naomi was here on a student visa. Acting was just an elective. After she finished her MBA, she went back to Japan."

"Do you know when that was?"

"It would have been May or June, three years ago."

At least a year before Katrina died. We'd been pretty sure Naomi was innocent, anyway, because of my vision, but having independent verification comforted me. "Thanks. I really appreciate you taking the time to talk to us."

"No problem." She leaned forward and lowered her voice. "Naomi is the kindest, most gentle person I've ever met. She runs a homeless shelter now. I don't know why you're asking questions, but if any member of the bridal party was involved with Katrina's death, I'd look at Mary or Priscilla."

My eyes widened. How had she figured out what we were doing? Were we so obvious?

Seeing my confusion, Sam stepped in. "Where were their tattoos? More tramp stamps like you and Katrina?"

Christie shook her head. "No way. They wanted to set themselves apart. They used to joke that the three of them looked so much alike, the tattoos were the only way anyone could identify them. That was before Prissy started dying her hair."

"What about the tattoos?" I tried hard to keep the urgency out of my voice, but we were so close to getting answers. I didn't want to get off track.

"Either Mary or Prissy got a vine wrapped around her ankle, I believe," Christie said.

I held my breath. Sam asked the all-important ultimate question. "And the other?"

"I'm pretty sure it was on her wrist."

The wrist. Just like the tattoo I'd seen when scrying Katrina's mirror. Now I knew: either Mary or Priscilla had killed her. Whichever of them it was wanted to take Kyle, Katrina resisted, and she got killed fighting back. I still didn't know exactly why either Mary or Priscilla would be so interested in a toddler, but my vision told me it had to do with his powers.

"Thanks, Christie. Listen, this is extremely important. Do you remember which one of them had the wrist tattoo?"

She thought for a long time before she answered. "I'm not sure. It was a long time ago. We got pretty drunk before going in, and I wasn't in the same room as either of them. At the wedding, I was focused on Katrina, not Mary and Priscilla. I haven't seen either of them since she died."

My disappointment must've been palpable because Sam leaned over and took my hand.

Christie spotted the gesture. Her eyes went from our locked hands to Sam back to me. "Sorry. I wish I could say something to help you find what you're looking for."

"It's okay," Sam said. "You've given us a lot of information. Thanks for taking the time."

Either Mary or Priscilla had killed Katrina. One of them was locked inside Destiny's Haven. But who was it?

CHAPTER SEVENTEEN

It was late when I finally made it back to Shady Grove. Too late to reach out to Geoff to give my condolences or to carefully ask probing questions to verify whether he may have killed his sister to steal her inheritance. Until I heard from the officers who were at the scene, it didn't matter. They'd said they call if they thought of any questions for me. Maybe I hadn't gotten any messages because Deborah killed herself, like the note said.

Bright and early Monday morning, I sent a video chat request to my friend Tiffaneigh. Tiffaneigh Pratt and I met on my first day at Maloney College when she stole my parking space, then my seat. We'd come a long way since then, even solving a murder together. Tiffaneigh knew about my powers, and her father was a police officer. More importantly, she'd stolen a key piece of evidence for me once, so she wasn't above getting her hands dirty in the name of the greater good. She might be willing to help me with a little undercover operation.

Instead of hello, she said, "What'd you get on the Molecular Chem. final?"

I grinned at her. "One hundred and two. Figured out the extra credit was a trick question. You?"

She sighed. "Same. What's up?"

Quickly, I outlined my plan and the role I hoped she would play. While speaking, I pulled out images of Destiny's Haven that I'd printed in Kevin's home office after dropping Kyle off at preschool this morning. Their website prominently showed the grounds, but I'd also found a couple of pictures of the common areas.

"This is it?"

"Not quite." I gave her a small smile before pulling out my big finale. "I went to City Hall on my way here and got the building plans plus an electrical map, so we can see the basic layout of the interior and get an idea of where the bedrooms are."

She faked a gasp. "Did you break into City Hall?"

"Um, no. I walked in, asked for the documents, and paid the fees," I said. "Are you sure you're the daughter of a cop?"

"I like to live dangerously," she said. "Anyway, I'm still impressed that you did all this legwork. What do you need me to do?"

It didn't take long for us to finish going over the details. She agreed to borrow her dad's car to drive out to Destiny's Haven after her last class of the day. I didn't want to take my Prius in case someone remembered seeing it. Her own car might be more fun to ride in, but people tended to see a vintage red Mustang with "QnTiff" on the plates and remember it. I certainly had. Of course, she'd been cutting me off at the time.

After we hung up, I made a quick trip to Let's Bake a Deal. Fortunately, the owner wasn't working and his much more pleasant sister manned the cash register. Tony had never forgiven me for trying to barter the cost of a cake the first time I came in. Come on. It was literally in the store's name. Anyway, baked goods were an excellent way to open doors, and I needed a favor.

Once back in the car, I drove through the middle of town toward the golf course. Kevin had a family membership so he could meet clients while Kyle and I used the pool, but that wasn't my intent. Instead, I drove around the block and parked in the driveway of a bubble-gum-pink house, so bright you needed sunglasses to look at it. To my great surprise, a moving van was parked on the street outside.

Before I lost my nerve, I walked up to the porch and rang the doorbell.

Thelma Reyes was the town gossip and a retired actress. For more than twenty years, she'd starred on *As the Hospital Guides Our Lives,* my new favorite daytime soap opera. Though she'd moved to Shady Grove a while ago, she never lost her theatrical nature. She reigned supreme over the coffee shop each morning before she went home to watch "her shows," gathering up as much information as she could about the locals and happily spreading it around to anyone who would listen. She also loved Tony's chocolate cake.

Not that I wanted her to know what Tiffaneigh and I were up to, but no one in town could match her for knowledge of makeup and disguise, which we would need to pull this off.

"Why, hello, Aluminum," Thelma said when she opened the door.

No one else in town, other than my brother, dared use my full name. For once, I didn't bother to correct her. "Good morning, Thelma. Do you have a few minutes? I brought you some cake."

"Of course, of course," she said. "What can I do for you?

I heard that you're in the market for a tea set, and I happen to have a gorgeous piece that was once used on the show. It was part of my house. When Dorothy Rose invited someone over for tea, you always knew something big was about to happen. When I retired, they said the tea set was so much a part of Dorothy Rose, I might as well keep it as a memento. You can't have the original, of course, but there are some replicas in my basement."

With effort, I stopped my mouth from dropping open. How did this woman know everything? As soon as she took a breath, I jumped in. "Thank you, but no. A friend and I are doing a skit for drama class. I was hoping you could help us?"

When I explained what I needed, giddiness radiated off of her. Thelma loved a good bit of gossip, but as I suspected, she also embraced the opportunity to feel useful. Working with me and Tiffaneigh behind the scenes to "write a skit" for drama class—and put us into disguises—had to be almost as good as being back on set for the day.

"Come in, come in!"

"Do you think you can turn me into someone else?" I asked as I followed her down the hall. "The teacher said I should look like a different person."

"With the right makeup and tools, anyone can transform into someone else. I'll fix you right up." She directed me to sit on the couch while she went to make tea. "By the time we're done, your own mother wouldn't recognize you."

While I waited, I asked, "Are you moving? I saw a van parked on the street outside."

"Don't be ridiculous, dear. They'll have to carry me out of this place in a body bag. Someone finally bought Earl's house."

Earl Parker, Thelma's next-door neighbor and long-time

boyfriend, had been killed at the beginning of this year. The house went to his brother, who was also Rusty's dad. For a while, Rusty thought about living there, but he'd decided he valued his privacy more than free rent.

"Oh, yeah? Do you know who's moving in?" I wasn't particularly interested in the answer, but Thelma must've had her nose pressed up against her kitchen window all day. She'd be dying to spill every little detail.

"Ellie Jackson bought it. She finally got tired of living with her daughter and grandkids. Not that I blame her. They've got three little boys now, and that's a lot of energy for one small house. Plus, her daughter just got a new job working for the mayor, and I heard that they're expecting Ellie to provide free babysitting all day. I bet she couldn't move out fast enough."

Thelma continued chattering on while I wondered if Ellie's daughter was aware that Mayor Banister had been through fifteen assistants since I moved to town less than two years ago. She also blackmailed the sheriff into arresting Olive for a murder she didn't commit, but that was another story.

Now that was a bit of gossip Thelma would love. It would be all over Shady Grove in minutes. Thelma liked to say that giving her hot news was the original "going viral." For now, my lips were sealed. Suffice to say that when the election rolled around, I'd be voting for the other guy.

No worries. Thelma didn't need anyone else to help her carry on a conversation. By the time she spun me around to face the mirror, I knew more about the personal lives of every resident of Shady Grove than I ever imagined needing to know. Then, at the sight of the stranger staring back at me out of the mirror, I promptly forgot it all.

Thelma had given me oily skin (how?), broadened my

nose, made my lips fuller, thickened my eyelashes, and even added a smattering of freckles. The hair was a wig, but she'd filled in my eyebrows the same color so they matched.

A slow smiled stretched across my face. This plan just might work.

CHAPTER EIGHTEEN

When Tiffaneigh stepped outside her house half an hour later, she stopped dead at the sight of me leaning against my car at the end of her driveway. "Holy guacamole!"

"Is that a good thing? Guacamole is delicious."

"Definitely good. I barely recognized you in that getup," she said. "Are you wearing false eyelashes?"

"I like how that's what you fixate on," I said, pointing. "I'm wearing fake eyelashes, a wig, fake boobs, colored contacts, lifts in my shoes, and butt implants. I didn't even know butt implants were a thing, and I'm wearing them. Plus about forty pounds of makeup."

"Thelma did a spectacular job." Tiffaneigh walked around me in a circle, looking me up and down. "Your butt looks amazing. Where can I get one of those?"

"Tell you what. We get what we need today, and they're yours." I took in her crisp white lab coat, black slacks with pleats so sharp they could cut paper, and shoes she must've borrowed from her mom. For once, her hair was pulled back in a sleek chignon instead of in twin black braids. She'd also piled on the makeup until she looked a good ten years older, which fit our cover story perfectly. "You look good, too."

"I know."

On the drive to Destiny's Haven, we reviewed the plan until we could both recite it without even thinking. Then, when I started to get nervous, Tiffaneigh quizzed me on the elements of the periodic table.

She took a long look at me after pulling into a parking space. "Last chance to back out."

"No. No way. I need to talk to whoever is in there. Whether it's Mary or Priscilla, it's time."

"Okay, then." She patted her hair one last time, pulled a pair of fake glasses out of her bag, and settled them onto her nose. "Let's do this, Titanium."

"That's not funny."

She smirked at me as she got out of the car and pulled a small rolling suitcase from the back. "Says you. Sorry, I couldn't resist. Okay, let's go. Amy and Tairagh."

Since we didn't know anyone else in the facility and Mary/Priscilla wasn't accepting guests, we couldn't sign in and enter the normal way. My initial plan had been to pretend to be doctors, but that required many more years of medical school than either of us could claim. We didn't have the knowledge and vocabulary to pull off that ploy if anyone questioned it. Even if we could, the facility probably had some way of verifying our credentials. After a lot of thought, we'd gone with something easier to fake: pharmaceutical reps.

Tiffaneigh even printed up some fake business cards, where I'd been prepared to just pretend I forgot to bring mine. I appreciated that she insisted on a unique spelling of her fake name rather than just going with the more common "Tara."

She led the way, partially because my knees were knocking together and partially because I didn't want anyone to look too closely at me. "Tairagh" would do most of the talking. She waltzed through the front door of the facility, pulling the roller bag behind her, looking straight ahead with the confidence of someone who knew exactly where they were going in life.

Harmony stood at the reception desk, just like the first time I'd been there, and she greeted us the same way.

"Good morning," Tiffaneigh said. "I'm Tairagh Carter and this is my associate, Amy. We're here from Reyes Pharmaceuticals, and we'd like to talk to your doctors about some exciting new options on the market."

Harmony rolled her eyes. "Salespeople go around the back. Come on, you should all know that by now."

"Sorry," Tiffaneigh said. "I just transferred from our Boston division. So, we go out the front door and—"

"To your car," Harmony said. "Come back next week. This is a closed facility, and we only accept sales pitches on Mondays."

Oh, no. We weren't leaving. Not after everything.

Tiffaneigh took a deep breath and launched into a story about what an extremely long day she'd had and how we were just covering for someone else, who had apparently gotten the dates and other information wrong...it was all very fascinating, since we'd practiced none of it and not a single word was true. I was so impressed, I almost forgot that she was giving me a chance to slip away.

Then movement down the hall caught my eye.

Mary/Priscilla peeked around the corner from the longer hallway leading to the sitting area. When we made eye contact, she put one finger to her lips in the universal

"Shh!" motion. Then she tilted her head toward a closed door and disappeared inside.

She couldn't possibly have recognized me, especially from twenty feet away. And yet, I'd have been willing to bet my associate's degree that she did. I didn't know how or why she'd appeared, but I wasn't about to throw away my shot.

I poked my head around Tiffaneigh to address Harmony. "I'm sorry to interrupt you, but is there a restroom I could use?"

"Down the hall to the right. You're not back in two minutes, I'll call security."

Getting chased out of the building by armed men for the second time in two visits didn't appeal at all. Instead of mentioning that I was already familiar with the process, I thanked her and headed off in the direction she'd pointed.

"Sorry about my *associate*." Tiffaneigh's voice followed me down the hall. "She's new. It's so hard to train good help these days."

I paused at the door long enough to see Harmony watching me and slipped inside. Hopefully, she wouldn't realize that I wouldn't be alone.

As expected, Mary/Priscilla waited for me inside the bathroom. "Hello, Aly."

A surprised gasp escaped me. "How did you know who I am?"

"You're not the only one in this family with powers," she said. "That's why Kyle is so strong, you know. He gets it from your side of the family and mine."

At the mention of my nephew, a chill went down my spine. "What do you know about Kyle?"

"Same as you," she said. "Same thing Katrina knew, if she'd been willing to admit it."

"Last time I was here, you told me you weren't Mary. Are you Priscilla?"

She blinked several times. "I see you've done your research."

I nodded. "I know that Mary and Katrina have a cousin named Priscilla, who bore a strong resemblance to both of them. I've seen the pictures. I know a bunch of you got matching tattoos in different spots. I know someone pretending to be Mary called me a few weeks ago, and I know you're checked into the rehab facility under her name, yet you say you're not her. Now I also know you've got some kind of psychic powers."

The sheer terror on this woman's face the last time I was here went a long way toward convincing me that she was telling the truth. But now, after poring over the images in the photo album for several hours, I thought I saw it. Mary's face was a bit more square, whereas Priscilla's face was an oval. This woman's eyes were hazel instead of brown. Minor distinctions, but enough to tell them apart.

"When you first said you weren't Mary, I thought you were talking about body-swapping."

She snorted. "Mary doesn't have that kind of power."

"I'm relieved to hear it. But then, what are you doing here?"

"Mary filed documents with the courts as Priscilla, claiming I'm so far gone on drugs that I think I'm her. She used her powers to get me involuntarily committed. Witnesses swore up and down that she's Priscilla Huntington, and I'm Mary Towne. I don't know if they even knew they were lying."

Mary was a witch, so I didn't know if Priscilla was talking about magical or non-magical powers of persuasion, but at the moment, it didn't matter. I only had a couple of minutes.

"Can't you leave? I thought this was a voluntary dry-out facility."

"Lots of people here checked in voluntarily. They get to come and go. I'm not one of them. Mary hexed the judge, and now I'm stuck here."

"But why would she do that?"

"Isn't it obvious?" Priscilla said. "As soon as I found out about Kyle's powers, I knew Mary was the one who killed Katrina."

After all this time, having someone confirm it felt like a thousand-pound weight getting lifted off my shoulders.

"How did you know?"

"Mary was talking about some big spell she wanted to do, how she didn't think she could work it on her own. She needed someone else she could draw on, and if they were related to her, that would make the spell more powerful. I offered to help, of course, but what I have is more intuition than anything else. I'm terrible at spells, other than really basic blessings and a couple of healing potions."

"Was Katrina a witch, too?"

She shook her head. "I don't think so. Our gifts don't affect everyone the same way, and her dad has zero magic in his blood. I could be wrong, but if she did have some power, I never saw it."

Based on what I saw in my vision, that fit. Everything this woman said made sense. We had so much to talk about. There were so many things I wanted to ask her.

At this point, though, only one question mattered. Before I did anything else, I needed to be one hundred percent positive whether she was telling the truth about who killed Katrina. "Can I see your tattoo?"

She blinked at me. "I'm sorry?"

"Your tattoo. You, Mary, Katrina, Christie, and Naomi all got them before the wedding, remember? An ivy vine twisted in various shapes, with buds?"

"Ohhh, that." She paused. "I'm sorry, Aly, I had mine covered up after Katrina died. Looking at it was just too painful."

My eyes darted to her wrists, but she wore one of those stupid long-sleeved workout shirts with thumbholes that covered everything. I mean, okay, those shirts were amazing when exercising or needing to be outside, but they sucked when I needed to look at the wrists of a person wearing one. "What did you get?"

"That's personal." She rolled up her sleeves, revealing smooth, perfectly clear skin. Not a tattoo, not a scar, not a sunburn or even a freckle. Totally bare. "But look. Mary's the one with the wrist tattoo."

Priscilla didn't have a wrist tattoo. The person who killed Katrina did. Even if she'd had it removed, there would probably be something remaining. Tattoo removal wasn't that perfect, was it? She was innocent.

Which only left Mary.

Finally, I knew the truth.

"Thank you," I whispered.

Everything else I wanted to say would have to wait, as I heard heels click-clacking down the hall toward the bathroom door and Tiffaneigh's voice calling out "Amy's" name.

"Look, I have to go. If Harmony finds out who I am, she'll call the cops. I brought you this." I pulled a tiny burner phone out of my back pocket and slipped it to her. "My number is pre-programmed. Text me anytime."

She slipped it into her bra. "Thanks. When will I see you again?"

"Hopefully soon. Kevin and I are going to figure out how to get you out of here so we can find Mary."

"What are you going to do once you find her? You can't exactly tell the police you're from a family of psychics."

I moved toward the door as she slipped into the stall to hide, and I moved toward the door. "I have no idea how, but I'm going to get justice."

"Aly." The seriousness in her voice made me stop and turn back. "Be careful. Mary's dangerous."

CHAPTER NINETEEN

By the time I got home, my head was spinning. The past few days had been extremely illuminating. With everything I'd learned, there was no longer any point in trying to hide my powers from Kevin. He needed to know what I'd found out and how. Maybe he could help me figure out what to do next.

Telling Kevin everything I'd learned also meant telling him about Kyle. There was no way around it. His three-year-old son had psychic abilities. Both Mary and Priscilla knew it. Professor Zimm saw it the day she met us. Katrina realized it before she died, although I wasn't sure exactly when. Sam had known as soon as Kyle told him where to find me in the woods that day.

For whatever reason, my nephew's abilities hadn't waited to manifest until he was twenty-one. Maybe it was a different gene mutation. Maybe he was just lucky, or it was because his power came from both sides of the family or boys revealed their powers sooner or he was more powerful than me. It didn't matter.

What mattered was Kevin and I were long overdue for

an honest conversation. He needed to know everything I'd been up to.

These thoughts whirled around in my head all through dinner, all the way up the stairs, during my entire bedtime routine with Kyle. The cool thing about hanging out with a three-year-old was that he didn't notice when my mind was somewhere else.

Finally, though, it was time. After giving Kyle eleven hugs, reading him seven stories, and taking him to the bathroom four times, I said goodnight and went downstairs. Kevin sat on the couch reading a book. I studied him for a minute. Although we had the same parents and grew up in the same house, there was so much we didn't know about each other. Kevin left for school when I was nine years old, and a person did a lot of learning and growing between nine and twenty. Not to mention, teenage boys weren't big on hanging around their kid sisters. He took care of me, and we loved each other in that "well, you're my brother so I have to" way, but we never really connected until I moved in.

More and more, I wondered if Kevin had known, or suspected, something that led him to ask me to move in instead of hiring a nanny. Mom and Dad had good state jobs in California, with pensions, so they weren't leaving the area any time soon. They weren't in a position to give it all up and move to New York to help with their grandchild. Bringing me in instead seemed like a great idea—I'd been looking to transfer from community college to a four-year school to finish my degree. Maloney College was a great school, and one I'd been eyeing even before Katrina died.

But now I wondered why he hadn't hired a nanny or au pair. Kevin had plenty of money, and surely a trained professional knew more about raising kids than I did. There was no reason to ask me to give up my life, was there? I was practically a stranger when Katrina died. Maybe he had some other reason for wanting me here. Shady Grove was a place where weird things happened, in a family where weird things happened.

Before I could figure out what to say, Kevin looked up. Goosebumps stood up on my arms. I wasn't afraid of my brother, but I wasn't ready for what this conversation might reveal.

"Do I have something on my face?" he asked.

"Huh?"

"You're staring," he said. "Everything okay with Little Man?"

"Yeah, he's fine. Made sure I kissed all of his stuffed animals before I left the room." The memory brought a whisper of a smile to my face, but I couldn't get distracted. I decided to ease Kevin into this conversation, see how things went. "Remember a few weeks ago, we were talking about Katrina, and you said Mary was her only close family?"

He thought for a minute. "Vaguely. Why?"

"What about Priscilla?"

"Her cousin?"

"Yeah."

He shrugged. "She was really closer with Mary. They were all friends, I guess, but Katrina wouldn't have spent time with Priscilla if they weren't related."

My eyes narrowed. "She was one of your bridesmaids. That's pretty close."

"I'm surprised you remembered that."

I actually didn't, but I wasn't ready to correct him yet. Kevin's shoulders eased back into place. "I see why you're confused. She was a last-minute replacement."

"Huh?"

"Mary pushed hard for Katrina to ask Priscilla to be in

the wedding party from day one, but she was going to school in Baltimore. We barely saw or talked to her. Katrina told Mary she'd rather ask a close friend, someone she saw every day. To be honest, it wasn't a big deal. I hadn't thought about it in years."

Weird that Christie hadn't mentioned another bridesmaid. It seemed like an important piece of information. Sure, maybe she forgot, but I made a mental note to send Christie a message later, just in case.

"What happened?" I asked.

"Mallory broke her leg skiing a couple of weeks before the ceremony, and she needed surgery. She wasn't confident on crutches yet, so she backed out. I told Katrina to ask you, but there was no time to get the dress altered. We went with Priscilla, who wore the same size."

Hmm. What a convenient "accident" for Priscilla. I made a mental note to find Mallory and ask her a few questions. But then the first part of what he said hit home. "You told her to ask me?"

"Of course. You're my baby sister. You were more annoying back then, but I still loved you."

I stuck my tongue out at him. Something he'd said prickled at my memory, so I bit back a biting retort to ask the more important question. "Did Mallory get a tattoo, too? Seems like if it was a wedding party thing, and she had to leave last minute, she might have still wanted one."

"No idea."

Well, fluorine. Another line of questions I couldn't pursue at the moment. If Christie were willing to talk to me again, though, she might remember. I'd send her a message once we finished this conversation. Which led me to the part of the discussion I'd been dreading since my twenty-first birthday.

I took a deep breath. It was now or never. Skipping the segue, I said, "Kev, I'm psychic."

Kevin did a spit take, which impressed me since he wasn't drinking anything. "What? Come on, Aly! What a ludicrous thing to say! You're psychic? Should I start calling you Miss Cleo now? Ha ha, you're so funny."

"Wow," I said. "For the sake of all your clients, I hope your poker face is better in court."

At least he had the good grace to blush after that terrible performance. "Did I go too far?"

"It's thicker than Kayne's ego in here."

With a sigh, Kevin stood up. "We need drinks for this. Come on."

I followed him into the kitchen and waited while he poured himself a scotch. He offered me one, but I shook my head. I grabbed some water instead and perched on a stool next to the island. "Why do I sense you already knew about me?"

"Because I did," he said. "Or at least, I suspected. What happened?"

"Many things," I said. "Starting the day I turned twenty-one, I've been getting visions. Of the past, not the future. Not always, but sometimes when I touch an object, I can see a peek into the life of a prior owner."

"That sounds like a cool power."

His tone made me forget what I'd been about to say. "It is, actually. Weird sometimes, but did you know Thelma stole her Daytime Emmy award?"

He choked on his whiskey. "I didn't, but that is hilarious. Good old Thelma."

"You didn't seem at all surprised to hear that I have visions. Do you get them, too?"

"Not visions, no. I see the truth."

Of all the things I'd expected him to say, that one never occurred to me. "You what?"

"I can see the truth. Well, more accurately, I can see lies. They come out of the speaker's mouth a different color than regular words. Which is how I know that you're not messing with me, and you believe what you're saying. That doesn't always mean what a person is telling me is factually accurate, but it's a strong indicator in most cases."

"Whoa. Hold up." I resisted the urge to slam my fists on the counter. "How could you not tell me? After everything we've been through?"

"You never told me, either," he pointed out. "You're a scientist, Aly. You've got an analytical mind. There was no point telling you something you weren't prepared to believe."

As much as I hated to admit it, he had a point. Even when that first vision hit, it took a few days to get my head around the idea of having superpowers. A few days, and a lot of use of the scientific method. Even as a psychic, I needed proof. "What about Mom and Dad?"

"We get it from Mom," he said. "She didn't want to tell you if she didn't have to. She told me everything about a week before my twenty-first birthday. I'd noticed, of course, that we never went to garage sales like my friends. Never visited antique stores. Mom doesn't even like hotels."

"That's right. She used to make comments about sleeping on other people's sheets," I said. "She'd bring her own when we had to travel."

"Exactly. Anyway, I walked in on her when she was having a vision. I didn't know what it was. She just—wasn't herself. Her eyes were glazed over, and this sound that wasn't her came from inside."

Whoa. Was that what I was like during a vision? I

should have Olive video me next time. "What did she see? Do you know?"

He shook his head. "She refused to talk about it. But I finally got her to admit to extra-sensory gifts. She thought maybe I'd have them, too, which may be part of what eventually made her crack."

"It could have been your awesome interrogation skills."

"Not then, it couldn't." He laughed. "On my birthday, I suddenly had this power, and it changed my life. Gave me a whole new direction. That's when I honed my techniques."

"That's why you became a lawyer? You must be great with the criminal stuff. How do you deal with guilty clients?"

"Everyone deserves a defense, Aly," he said gently. "It's a Constitutional right for the guilty and the innocent. Besides, I'm amazing at detecting lies on cross-examination."

"I guess you would be." Something occurred to me. "Hold on! So you knew every time I wasn't entirely truthful with you?"

"Aly."

I squirmed under the intensity of his gaze.

"You told me you thought you were wearing earbuds when you weren't. A person doesn't exactly need to be psychic to recognize that lie."

He had a good point, so I changed the subject. "Does that mean you know about Kyle, too?"

"Not the specifics. He's too young to ask. Kids don't know what a lie is until they're older, so I wouldn't necessarily sense anything from him even if he told me the sky is purple. Either way, I've always known there was a good chance he would develop powers."

"He already has them. Kyle saved my life a few weeks ago. Well, sort of."

"What are you talking about?"

I told him how Tiffaneigh and I had gotten locked in the shed, trying to make it sound like a weird accident. Predictably, he interrupted at least three times to lecture me about the folly of solving murders on my own. I reminded him gently that the Shady Grove police could use help from someone with superpowers before diverting back to my story.

"Kyle knew exactly where to find me. Even if Tiffaneigh and I hadn't escaped on our own, Sam would have been there minutes later."

"You're saying Kyle can find lost people?"

I shook my head. "I don't think so. Remember the first day of classes? He gave me his dump truck for luck." For the first time, I wondered if Kyle had known the type of luck I would need when he handed me the tiny vehicle. Unfortunately, because he was three, I wasn't sure how to ask him. "He must have remembered. I don't know. When I got lost, I had that truck in my backpack. Kyle told Sam where to go, and he was right. There's no other way he could have known."

"Wow." Kevin blew out a breath. "All this time, I've been hoping he would escape the family gift."

His phrasing made my lips twitch. "That brings me to the third thing we need to talk about: the killer wasn't after Katrina. She wanted Kyle."

"She? You can't possibly know who did it, much less their gender or motive."

"Actually, I can. I found Katrina's mirror. Why did you hide it?"

He narrowed his eyes for a minute, thinking. "The

hallway mirror? Kyle was playing ball in the house, and I was worried he'd break it. That's an expensive mirror, and Katrina loved it."

I blew out a breath. "So it wasn't to keep me from finding it?"

"Why would I hide a mirror from you?"

"You didn't want me to know how Katrina died," I reminded him.

"Until about twelve seconds ago, I had no reason to think a mirror would be any use in figuring it out."

"Good point. Anyway, I used the mirror. I asked it to show me what happened."

"You can do that? Wow."

"Apparently so," I said with a modest shrug. "I'm still learning the limits of my powers. But it worked. I saw Katrina's death."

Quickly, I outlined everything the mirror, along with my subsequent investigation, had told me. I even sheepishly admitted to going through his storage unit, although I skipped Sam helping me try on the wedding dress.

Kevin's eyes widened. "Mary killed her sister? I can't believe it. They were so close."

"I don't have all the details, but if Mary has the rose vine tattoo on her wrist, it was her."

He looked so lost, I hugged him. Then I went to the sink to give him some space and get us both some water.

He accepted his gratefully. "Priscilla didn't come around by herself much, especially after Kyle was born. They both disappeared after Katrina died. It wasn't that surprising, though. Mary went into a total downward spiral, and I guess I figured Priscilla was with her."

"You said a while back that Mary thought *you* killed

Katrina. But you also said you can see the truth. Could you tell if she sincerely believed what she was saying?"

"No. We have to be face-to-face, and she accused me over the phone. At the funeral, she seemed legitimately broken up. We didn't talk about the details of Katrina's death."

"She could have killed her sister and felt bad about it."

"Exactly. And I never saw Priscilla after Katrina died. She didn't come to the funeral."

Huh. Here I'd thought I didn't remember seeing her because she and Mary looked similar, and I didn't know either of them well enough to tell them apart at the time. I'd had other things on my mind. "Why wasn't she there?"

"I don't know."

"If Priscilla is telling the truth, Mary killed Katrina. Then she got Priscilla committed, sent me a cursed rocking horse, and went into hiding. Apparently, she wanted Kyle to help her do some kind of spell."

"Kyle was only two when his mother died. What could he possibly have helped with?" Kevin asked.

"Priscilla said Mary wanted to tap his power. He's strong."

"Poor Katrina died saving him." Kevin's eyes shone. "I should have been there. I should have saved her."

"You couldn't have known." I hugged him. "If you'd been there, Mary might have come back later, or she might have killed you both and taken Kyle. You never know."

"You're right," he said. "I wonder why she left him behind that day."

"I don't know. My best guess is that she was horrified to realize what she'd done. She probably didn't mean to hurt Katrina." I shook my head. "I'm so sorry."

"Thank you. And thank you for telling me."

"Thank you for finally trusting me with the truth."

"I should have told you sooner," he said. "I'm sorry. But I can make it up to you."

"How?"

"I can go to Destiny's Haven, talk to the woman who lives there. See if she's lying."

I jumped to my feet. "Let's go!"

He chuckled. "Calm down. We can't go now. She's still in lockdown. But let me do some digging tomorrow, get the paperwork I need to reinstate her visitor's privileges. Then I'll go. Alone."

"Nope. I've been working on this for months. I'm going with you," I insisted.

"I don't want to put you in danger."

"As long as Kyle's the target of a powerful witch, I'm in danger. So are you. You don't have to protect me. I'm not a little kid anymore."

"You'll always be my baby sister." He kissed the top of my head. "I love you, Aly."

"I love you, too, Kelvy," I said. "Just don't go trying to suppress any more superpowers or I'll tell everyone your real name."

"You wouldn't dare, Aluminum," he said. "Try it, and I'll tell Sam that you've drawn Aly Green with hearts all over your notebooks."

I suppressed a smile as I left the room, shaking my head. Family.

CHAPTER TWENTY

My talk with Kevin made me feel much better. Together, maybe the two of us could figure out where Mary had gone and finally bring her to justice.

Meanwhile, it was time to finish taking care of Miriam Peabody's estate. Although the sale occurred only a few days ago, it felt like weeks. The moving van full of her belongings had arrived on Sunday while Sam and I were in New Jersey, interviewing Christie. Barry paid the movers to unload, so Olive didn't need our help for that, but with everything that had been going on, I hadn't had the time or the energy to finish the job.

The items in that moving van had homes, and Olive depended on me to help get them inventoried and into the store so we could sell them. Sure, I was only a part-time employee, but she shouldn't be moving and lifting heavy objects all day alone. Especially with no one around if she got hurt. Wednesday morning, I showed up at Missing Pieces bright and early, carrying a latte from On What Grounds? in one hand and a double espresso with cinnamon-flavored whipped cream in the other. Julie had recently started testing out new drink flavors on Olive. I had my doubts about this one, but as long as I didn't have to try it, I kept my mouth shut.

Olive and I both thought Miriam had been trying to contact me through her belongings, and that was why they sent off such strong vibes. If that was the case, I should be able to unpack and put everything else away with zero unwanted visions now that Deborah was dead. The key to avoiding visions was not to use anything in its intended manner. If that failed, well, this was a great time to practice suppressing things I didn't have any need or desire to see.

When I arrived, the door to the storage room stood open. Olive sat inside, sorting items as she hummed to herself, looking as happy as a kid in a candy store.

"Hello, dear! Any luck?"

Gleefully, I filled her in on all the things that had happened since we parted on Saturday. I ended with, "Now that I've solved two murders in the past three days, I'm here to help. Where do you need me?"

She pointed toward a clothes rack to my left. "Those are all going out on the main floor for sale. You should be able to price most of them without my help."

"I'm on it!"

She grinned at me.

"What?"

"Nothing, I just love seeing you in such a good mood."

"Of course, I'm in a good mood. I'm finally making progress on Katrina's case. Okay, sure, we don't know where Mary is—but I'm pretty sure it was her. Kevin and I are working together on a plan. Also, Sam likes me back."

"Told you so."

I stuck my tongue out at her. "I should always listen to you. Anyway, I'm so happy, I'm buzzing."

With that, I dove into the job. However, it didn't take long for me to realize that the vibrant energy coursing through my veins wasn't coming from within. It had started as soon as I walked into this room, and more importantly—it initially hit me when I entered Miriam's house. This wasn't the excitement from my talk with Kevin or at learning Deborah wasn't going to get away with murder. Someone or something had information, and it was screaming for me to hear it.

The air moved around me. The psychic waves were so strong I could practically see them floating by.

This was getting ridiculous. Miriam's possessions had shown me her death already. Justice had been served when Deborah killed herself. Miriam should be happily starting her new life in paradise, surrounded by men who looked like the Hemsworth brothers. By loudly counting the elements of the periodic table in my head, I forced the sound away.

Or at least, I tried. With each item I priced and put away, every object Olive pulled from the boxes and sorted, the vibrations grew stronger. By the time she emptied the last box, I was ready to tear my hair out.

"What do you want from me?" I yelled. Spinning in a circle, I stomped my feet, glaring at one box after the next. "I found your killer! I can't bring you back. Go into the light! Leave me alone!"

"Shh." Olive wrapped one arm around my shoulders. Her familiar patchouli and rose scent immediately calmed me. "Everything is going to be okay."

I sighed and leaned against her. "I don't understand. What is happening? I've never met objects that were so persistent. Is this how it's going to be as my powers get stronger? I can't work here if antiques start shouting at me all the time. Unless you want to find me some psychic noise-canceling headphones."

She tapped her chin thoughtfully. "Now there's an idea."

"If you make me a tinfoil hat, I quit."

"Would I do that to you?"

"Yes." I grinned at her for a brief second. "But seriously, what do we do?"

"It seems to me that Miriam's belongings are still trying to tell you something," Olive said.

"But what?"

"Maybe Miriam had some other unfinished business," Olive said. "She and Barry were talking about getting married, right? She could want an opportunity to say goodbye."

"Gloria thought he was planning to propose. I don't know if he ever did. But I'm not a medium, Olive. I can't pass messages between them. If she wants to say good-bye, I'm not the answer."

"True, but Miriam wouldn't necessarily know that. That's the problem with spirits. It could be almost anything."

"She's worried that she left the iron on?"

"Don't get fresh with me, young lady." She thought for a moment. "What was Barry saying about treasure?"

"Geoff was convinced Miriam's late husband buried a fortune somewhere in the house. In my vision, Deborah and Miriam were talking about how Miriam planned to move out soon. At the time, I thought she was moving into a home or something. I thought Deborah killed her to stop the sale."

"Right." Olive said, "Remember when we were searching the house, Geoff was banging on the walls?"

"Do you think all of these items are telling me there

really is treasure hidden in the house? They want me to find it? And what...return it to its rightful owner?"

"Sounds like a job designed for the two of us."

"We make a good team."

"That we do." Olive squeezed my hand. "I'm glad I hired you."

"Me, too." I glanced down at our clasped hands, the way the light glinted off Olive's engagement ring. A thought floated by, just out of my grip. "Whoa. Hold on."

"Are you having another vision?"

"No, more of a memory," I said. "Tell me something. How well do you know Barry?"

Olive paused in the middle of unzipping a garment bag. "I've been friends with his son since college. Barry introduced me to Maria."

As much as that made me want to thank Barry for bringing love—and by extension, Sam—into Olive's life, that certainly made my next question much stickier. "But how well do you *know* him? Really?"

"Aly? What are you getting at?"

I heaved a sigh. "I'm trying to think who else could have killed Miriam. What are the common motives? Love, revenge, money. We thought Deborah killed Miriam for money, but that doesn't seem to jive with her killing herself. Then I started thinking about love."

"And Barry was in love with Miriam."

"Gloria claimed they'd been secretly dating and someone saw him picking out rings last month. But no one I talked to mentioned that Miriam was recently engaged." I waved a piece of paper in the air. "Her obituary says that she's survived by one niece and one nephew. No fiancé or loving partner. There's no engagement ring in the inventory Barry sent us."

"I don't remember seeing one on Saturday, either," Olive said. "I spent a lot of time looking at jewelry, but I didn't get to the table until after the sale started. They could have sold it. Or maybe Deborah gave it back to Barry after Miriam died. After all, they'd only been engaged a couple of weeks. Assuming she said yes."

"Maybe," I said. "Or maybe she turned him down, and he killed her."

Olive barked out a laugh. "Don't be ridiculous. Barry wouldn't hurt a fly."

"You're sure about that?" I paused. "Don't get me wrong, Olive. I like the guy. I'm grateful he called us in and trusted us with such a sensitive job. But someone killed Miriam, and I'm increasingly sure it wasn't Deborah."

"You don't believe Deborah killed herself?"

"It's just too...pat," I said. "Too perfect. It doesn't make any sense. Especially that note. 'It's over. I'm sorry.'? Four words? That could have been the start of anything. She could have been writing out song lyrics or apologizing to a colleague for being late. Heck, that could have been a note from Miriam to Barry, breaking up with him."

Saying the words aloud solidified the ideas in my head. It was easy to think the case was solved, that Miriam had been avenged. But I'd been ignoring the fact that Deborah didn't have a motive to kill herself. Sure, she'd been stopped from boarding the plane, but there were many ways out of New York City. Boats left the docks daily, and we had these new-fangled things called cars. If Deborah had started driving right after leaving the airport on Sunday morning, she'd be in Mexico by now.

At the same time, even if Barry killed Miriam in a fit of rage for rejecting his proposal, he didn't have any motive for killing Deborah. Not unless she'd figured him out somehow. Maybe he went after her to get the ring back?

With a frustrated huff, I turned back to the stuff to be inventoried and put away. Olive went to On What Grounds? to get more coffee. I moved on to the seven hundredth box (or so it felt like), which contained a collection of first edition novels, some dating back fifty years. I opened the first one, ran my finger down the spine, flipped through a few pages.

I sat in the house, a book in my lap, looking at the garden through the window. A blue bird flew by, landing on one of the many feeders.

That was it. Short, and to the point. One of the weirdest visions I'd had to date. Visions typically showed something important in the life of the person who had owned an object. What momentous event came about when Miriam read *Ulysses?* Maybe she realized she preferred short, funny stories about geeky amateur detectives. Or maybe it was nothing. With a mental shrug, I piled the books on a cart Olive had brought in for this purpose and moved onto the next box.

Carton number two contained some old china plates and bowls. The same lovely rose and green pattern as my gorgeous, poisoned tea set. Too bad I didn't have a use for a full dinner service. Or a kitchen of my own. I should buy it anyway, store it in Kevin's basement until I needed it. When I pulled out one of the plates to admire the way the light gleamed off the pattern, again, the world faded away again.

I sat at the dining room table, a plate of lasagna in front of me. The tantalizing odor tickled my nose, making my mouth water. A knife and fork clinked against a plate nearby. Someone coughed.

Again, the vision ended abruptly. What was going on?

Wiping a bit of drool from my mouth, I sat back on my heels, gazing around the room. So much stuff. I shook my head. Olive would be back soon; I could ask her about these random visions. A box of old baby toys showed someone, presumably Miriam, rocking a little boy. Since the Peabodys only had a daughter, I wondered if it was Geoff, but my vision didn't say. A vase sent me a vision of Miriam walking down the hall past it.

One mundane vision after the next hit me while I unpacked. What was happening?

By the time Olive returned carrying a vanilla latte for me and something that looked like a creamsicle for her, I was sitting on a stool, slowly beating my head against the top of a large box.

"What's wrong?"

I explained the boring, constant visions coming from everything I touched. "It's too much. I have these powers, and it could be so amazing and I could help so many people. But I can't make them *work*."

"Listen. You do help people," she said. "You found Earl's killer, and Professor Zimm's. Police wouldn't have solved those crimes without your help."

"True, I guess."

"You *know*. I'd probably still be in jail if it weren't for you. Never forget that, Aly, because I won't."

Impulsively, I hugged her. "And I'll never forget all you've done for me. Thanks."

"You're welcome. Let's get back to work."

I groaned. "What's the point? Apparently everything that was near Miriam when she died is somewhere else. I'm only seeing one completely irrelevant memory after the next. Was she alone with her rooster collection?"

"Was there a common thread in the visions? Something being shown over and over?"

"I wanted to pinch myself in all of them to stay awake."

"Stop," Olive said. "Close your eyes. Think about your first vision of Miriam, the day she died. What do you see?"

"She's in her living room. The tea set is on the coffee table. Two full cups, one with bright red lipstick on the rim."

"Deborah's?"

"I don't think so. It's not her color."

"Is there anything else on the table?"

I wrinkled my forehead as if that would help me focus, and oddly, it did. "A brown leather handbag."

"Perfect," Olive said. "Did you notice Deborah's purse at the sale? She wasn't carrying one that I saw."

I shook my head as I opened my eyes. "No."

"That's okay. There's a box of purses in the corner. I went through it earlier, tagging items for sale. Let's see if we can find the one from your vision."

It didn't take long. Olive had sorted the bags by color, style, and size, with the largest on the bottom. All we had to do was dig. Before I knew it, I emerged from the box, the strap of the large purse from my vision clutched in my grasp.

Punching the air over my head, I cheered. The bag swung in an arc and hit me in the face. A yelp escaped me.

Amusement filled Olive's voice, but she managed to keep a straight face. "Are you okay?"

"Embarrassed but okay. A good reminder not to celebrate yet."

The brown leather bag contained about forty compartments. If this was the bag Miriam used the day she died, someone had already emptied it of her personal items. That was fine with me. I didn't have any use for half-used lipsticks, used tissues, receipts, or any of the other trash typically found in women's purses. I had to dig through Thelma's bag once, and it was like opening Pandora's box. The memory made me shiver.

Putting the bag on my shoulder, I walked up and down the length of the room as if window shopping. Nothing happened. I pulled the tab on the zipper, pretended to extract a wallet, and put it back. Still no vision. But it occurred to me that there was more than one way to find out what secrets a purse contained.

Holding it upside down, I shook the bag. Something clinked inside.

"A-ha!"

"Did you find something?" Olive asked.

Cocking my head, I shook the bag again. "Loose change caught in the lining?"

"Is that a thing?"

"Depends on how old the bag is. If there are holes in it, sure." With one hand, I felt around in the various pockets. After a minute, my fingers closed around a piece of cool metal. "Hmm."

"Is that a good hmm?"

"Probably nothing. A pocket." Gripping the zipper, I pulled. It stuck at one point, but I coaxed it back into place before trying again. On my third try, it finally opened enough for me to stick a finger inside. At the bottom of the pocket sat a small, flat, item. Without seeing it, it was impossible to be sure, but it felt like metal.

Finally, I pulled out the object. A silver house key.

CHAPTER TWENTY-ONE

For a long moment, I stared at the object in my hand as if I could will it to convey whatever information Miriam wanted me to have. My powers unfortunately didn't work that way. I didn't have a telepathic connection to the dead.

"Is that what I think it is?" Olive asked.

I nodded. "It has to be, right? Miriam's been sending me one vision after another, then she led me to her purse so I would find her house key. There must be something in her house she wants me to find before it's sold."

"Hold on, hold on," Olive said. "Let's not jump to any conclusions. We don't know that's Miriam's house key. It could go to a garden shed or a pool house or Deborah's apartment or her neighbor who asked her to water the plants."

"There's only one way to find out. If this key opens any door on that property, I want to know about it. If it belongs to someone else, well, I've only lost the time driving out there."

She held out her hand. "Or I could just tell you."

Oh, duh. I dropped it into her open palm.

"I should probably lie for your own protection," Olive said, her eyes closed. "But this key belongs to Geoff. Given his relationship to Miriam, I'd guess it's because he is Deborah's heir and the house would have gone to her if she were still alive. It could also be the key to his place in Manhattan."

"It's a single key, though. If he lives in a building, there would be a separate key for the outer door."

"True. Do you think there's still evidence inside the house? That Miriam's belongings are trying to lead you to it?"

Something had been percolating in the back of my mind for a couple of days. Finally, I spoke the words aloud. "I can't shake the idea that Miriam's ghost is trying to tell me something. Is that ridiculous?"

Olive said, "I can't tell you ghosts aren't real, because I don't know. It's certainly within the realm of possibility."

"There's something in that house. Someone or something wants me to find it."

"What do you think it is?"

"I have no idea," I said. "A new will, maybe?"

"Either that, or it wasn't Deborah you saw in your vision at all," Olive said.

Her words stopped me in my tracks. "What?"

"Who benefits from Deborah's death the most?"

"Geoff, I guess. Unless she had a will, he'll inherit everything as her closest relative." The word *everything* echoed in my head as I spoke. I said it again. "Including the house."

"The house that he's convinced contains hidden treasure."

"Killing Miriam would certainly make it easier for

Geoff to get into the house to search if she didn't want him around. We know he was looking."

"But how?" I asked. "Deborah killed Miriam. I saw it. When she realized we were on to her, she killed herself."

"You said before that it didn't make sense for Deborah to kill herself. Maybe she didn't." Olive wrinkled her forehead. "Has one of your visions ever been wrong?"

"How would I know?"

"Good point."

She thought for a moment. "Deborah and Geoff are twins, right?"

"Yeah."

"Why would Miriam leave everything to Deborah and not split any part of her estate between them?"

"From what other people have said, she thought he would squander her money on hare-brained schemes."

"How do you think Geoff felt about that? About the idea that he wasn't responsible enough to be trusted with a fortune?"

Anyone would be insulted to learn that one of their relatives thought they shouldn't have money because they couldn't be trusted to handle it responsibly. Would that anger drive him to kill?

"Based on the way Geoff and Deborah bickered at the estate sale, I'd say he wasn't thrilled," I said. "According to Lindsay, he was obsessed with his aunt's money. It sounded like he was constantly trying to get her to invest in some hot new business idea. Deborah said Miriam didn't like Geoff, but I think she was just trying to bug him."

"As siblings do."

"I have no idea what you're talking about," I said innocently. "But a sibling rivalry isn't a reason to kill someone."

"You're not thinking like a killer," Olive said. "If Geoff

felt slighted or angry, that could give him a motive to kill—not just his aunt, but Deborah, for taking away what he would have seen as his chance to inherit."

"You think he killed them both."

"Let's just say it's hard for me to believe that Deborah would kill herself just because she got stopped from boarding a plane. Even if she thought police were onto her, she had more than enough money to make a getaway."

"That's a good point," I said. "Plus, her brother worked in horror films. Geoff could have helped her with a disguise if she just wanted to get out of town."

"He also could have made himself up to look like Deborah to get close to Miriam. They're twins."

"You think it was Geoff that I saw in my vision?" I mulled that over and over. Thanks to Thelma, I now knew it wouldn't be that difficult to change Deborah's features into Geoff's. Miriam had terrible eyesight. They had different hair and eye colors, but wigs and colored contacts weren't exactly hard to come by. "What about the voice? I heard Deborah talking to Miriam in my vision."

"You didn't even know Geoff existed at that point," she reminded me. "And how much time had you spent talking to Deborah?"

"About eight seconds," I admitted. "You think he could've fooled me?"

"I think there's more to this story than either of us is aware."

"You're right," I said, already moving to grab my keys. "And Miriam is telling me the answer is on her property somewhere. I've got to go."

CHAPTER TWENTY-TWO

Three feet from the door, Olive caught me. "Aly, stop! You can't run off half-cocked."

"I can't stay here. Watching Miriam's belongings send me one boring vision after the next is making my head spin. I can't think."

"You could go home, rest, take the night off. Call the police and tell them your suspicions."

"All of my suspicions are based on my psychic powers," I said. "I've talked to the Lunar Heights police, and they think I'm hilarious. But listen. The house has been empty for a couple of days. If Geoff is looking for treasure, that's going to be a powerful draw."

"You're not helping your case."

"Okay, then. Call Geoff. Offer him a job. Ask him to send over his portfolio because we need someone to make props for when we decorate the store for Halloween. He'll be busy for hours getting it together."

"In five months?"

"All the big places prepare early," I said. "Look, if I get to the house and there's any sign of him, I'll leave."

"You're crossing your fingers behind your back."

I wasn't, only because she would see me. "I'm a big girl. But I have to go. Miriam's belongings aren't going to let me rest until we figure this out, and you can't sell them until they quiet down."

She sighed. "I don't like this."

"That's why you had Maria teach me self-defense, right?"

Finally, she let me go. I wouldn't have been surprised in the least if she called the Lunar Heights police to report a break-in at the Peabody house, but at least she didn't try to physically stop me. Olive had been married to a self-defense expert for twenty-five years. Sure, Maria gave me a few lessons over the past few months, but no way I could overpower Olive.

A few hours later, I stepped onto the front porch of the Peabody estate. Before moving toward the front door, I surveyed the grounds. The curtains were drawn and the driveway mostly empty, but otherwise, the house looked the same as it had on Saturday.

Miriam must've had at least three acres, which left a lot of space for someone to hide. The gardens alone stretched practically as far as my eye could see. I spotted at least one shed that could hide evidence, a pool house, and a far-off building that appeared to be a stable. Since no one mentioned horses, I assumed it was currently unoccupied. With no idea what I'd be looking for, I was starting to wish I'd packed a sleeping bag.

Only one way to get through this, though. Start with the main house and go from there.

This time when I entered, the house didn't give off any sort of vibe or energy. That actually made sense, because my powers worked with a person's belongings, and all of

Miriam's items had been removed. Still, I was a little surprised. If there wasn't anything in the house to tell me what really happened to Miriam and Deborah, why had Miriam directed me to come here?

As I walked from room to room, a sense of despair descended. How could I get a vision of Miriam if she never saw or touched any of these things? Finally, I moved toward the kitchen. People usually left their appliances when a house was sold, so if Miriam did any cooking, that was the only thing I could think of.

The kitchen looked more or less the same as I remembered: tons of counter space, lots of granite, gorgeous white cabinets that Kyle would mark constantly, and large stainless-steel appliances. A huge fridge, two built-in ovens, plus a separate stove top, a giant sink, and a dishwasher that appeared to require a college degree to operate.

The counters were bare except for a lighter sitting next to the fridge. I recognized it instantly as Barry's. Poor guy should put that thing on a string. A tiny voice reminded me of how he said he'd be better off if people stopped returning it, but then I remembered that it held sentimental value for him. Since his office was on my way back to the highway, I stuck it in the outside pocket of my leggings. At least this wouldn't be a completely fruitless mission.

Speaking of fruit, I turned my attention back to the kitchen. Cooking was not my thing. An avid viewer of MasterChef Junior, Kyle made most of our meals. I tended to burn kiddie foods like chicken nuggets and instant mac 'n cheese, so no one minded this division of labor.

My search began at the sink. A thick, plush pink mat with roses sat on the floor in front of it. After positioning myself on the mat, I turned on the water and pretended to be washing a dish.

Nothing happened.

Turning off the sink, I moved to the fridge. Although I'd expected it to be empty, I found half a carton of ice cream in the freezer. After opening and closing about seventeen drawers, I concluded that the silverware had been removed along with everything else. That made sense, since it was part of the estate sale, but didn't help me. I mimed taking a bite of the ice cream using one finger as a "spoon." Nothing happened.

With a guilty look around, I tried scooping out a bite and popping it into my mouth. Delicious, but nothing. Too delicious, actually. Miriam had been dead for weeks. Apparently the uber-rich could afford fancy fridges that avoided freezer burn. Why was this even here? Whoever cleaned the place should've tossed it.

"Help me help you, Miriam," I said to no one. My voice echoed through the empty room.

Might as well see if rinsing my finger and pretending to put it in the dishwasher triggered anything. It didn't, and I wasn't surprised at all. This had been a dumb idea. I didn't have any more idea what Miriam wanted to show me than I had when I left Shady Grove. But I was here, so I might as well keep looking.

When I started pressing random buttons on the oven, I realized I'd hit rock bottom. What was next, pretending to bake brownies? They'd probably fake burn. I opened the door and peeked inside. Nothing but a pilot light, the unpleasant smell of gas. Hastily, I closed it. I didn't realize they made partially electric gas ovens, but Miriam's had a billion buttons and nothing to help me figure out what any of them did. I pressed a few. At one point, I thought I heard a click, but no visions.

Clearly, Miriam's kitchen didn't have anything to tell me.

Hadn't Gloria said Lindsay's father put in a finished basement? Maybe someone hid something down there.

Inside the mudroom, I found a door pointing toward the interior of the house. It was closed, but the latch wasn't locked, which hopefully meant the basement was used fairly regularly and not full of mice and dust. When Olive and I came through here the day of the estate sale, I hadn't noticed it. A switch just inside the door illuminated a set of carpeted steps leading underground. The landing at the bottom turned, so I couldn't see anything else, but something told me I'd come to the right spot.

At the foot of the stairs, I stopped dead at the sight of a sleeping bag on top of a massive air mattress. Beside it was a battery-powered radio, an e-reader, a cooler, and stacks of baked goods in cartons. The cookies in the top box were still soft. Like the ice cream, this stuff was out of place. Someone had been here.

I should go. Someone had broken in or was camping out here. The room appeared empty at the moment, but I had no way of knowing if or when they'd be coming back. Was it one person or several? Geoff had been looking for treasure, so he seemed the most likely suspect.

Part of me wanted to turn and run. But the driveway was empty. Whoever was here must've left. I just needed to find my evidence and get out of here before they returned.

Shivering in the cold air, I started to move deeper into the underbelly of the house when my foot caught on the edge of the blanket. I tripped, pin wheeling my arms and barely catching myself. Phew.

Leaning down, I adjusted the blanket. A leather-bound corner sticking out from under the pillow caught my eye. I tugged at it, revealing the same book I'd found under the bed where we found the "dead body" on the day of the sale. What was it doing here?

I hadn't really looked at the book at the time, so I examined it now to see why someone brought it to the basement. The dark cover was unmarked, telling me instantly this was not a novel. Inside the front cover, someone had stamped *Property of Liam Peabody.* Cramped handwriting slanted up across the unlined paper. A diary. I was holding Liam's diary. It was old, the earlier pages stiff and yellowing.

Small, cramped writing filled the lines, a perfect match for the torn piece of paper that I'd found on the floor of Deborah's apartment. How had it gotten there? When was it removed from this book?

I flipped through the book, looking for the rest of that entry, but all I found was a spot near the end where an entire page was missing. Whatever the missing entry said about Lindsay Grant would remain a mystery.

The next page jumped out at me, though.

THERE'S SOMETHING WRONG WITH MY WIFE. SHE'S BEEN POSSESSED BY THE DEVIL. MIRIAM KNOWS THINGS SHE SHOULDN'T KNOW, HEARS PEOPLE WHO AREN'T THERE. GOD HELP US ALL.

I wondered what happened to make Liam believe his wife was possessed, but it didn't matter. Like Olive and I suspected, she had powers. For whatever reason, she'd apparently chosen not to tell her husband. It must be tough to keep that kind of secret from a spouse, but if he thought she was possessed, I didn't blame her. At least Miriam's secret explained why I was getting messages from her now.

My powers weren't evolving to speak to the dead. For some reason, that information comforted me. Communicating with ghosts was cool and all, but I liked knowing what was going on. If my powers could randomly mutate, that freaked me out more than discovering they existed.

Returning to the book, I flipped back to see if the early entries told me anything useful. The binding fell open to a creased page, one that had clearly been read and re-read many times. At first glance, I couldn't tell why. Time had faded the ink and made things difficult to read, but someone with good light and a lot of free time could probably decipher it. Whatever Liam had written here must have been interesting enough for Geoff to pore over it.

I didn't have the luxury of sitting here until I figured out what the book said. Luckily, I had something better: an extra-sensory ability to get information from objects. With a glance at the door to make sure no one was coming, I sat on the bed and pulled the book into my lap. Then I pinched my finger and thumb together as if holding a pen and started to "write".

My diary lay open on the wooden desk in front of me. A pen scratched across the pages, moving quickly and carefully. Small, precise letters filled about two-thirds of the page.

My lawyer says I need a better hiding place. Miriam wants to dig up the yard for a garden, and she'll have a conniption if she finds stolen goods. After a lot of thought, I decided the best thing to do was hide my booty in plain sight. We've got all that space in the basement. If we put in the over-priced wine cellar Miriam wants, no one would ever notice an extra storage space built into the back wall.

Lloyd's a builder, and he'd certainly help me. He keeps his mouth shut, too.

With a start, I shut the book. Geoff had been right all along. There really was treasure buried in the basement of this house. At least when Liam installed the wine cellar. It had been several years—who knew if anything was still there. Either Liam or Miriam could have taken the stolen goods long ago. But it sounded like Miriam didn't know about it.

My footsteps echoed on the stone floor as I followed the massive basement about a hundred feet down the hallway. At the end, I found the wine cellar, enclosed by stone walls lined top to bottom with those diamond-shaped boxes. At first glance, there had to be over two hundred, although there wasn't time to count. All the empty racks must've once held enough wine to pay for my entire college education and Kyle's. No more, though. Now everything was empty, creating an echo chamber for footsteps. It was even colder in this back room than the front of the basement.

The only other thing in the room was a pub-height island with four stools. Maybe for tastings? Weird that they didn't take the wine upstairs, but if you didn't mind freezing, this would be an okay place to hang out. Someone had left a bottle of vodka on the counter. A glance at the label told me it was the good stuff—Kevin only brought that brand out for special occasions. Because of the price or the high proof, I wasn't sure. Maybe both.

I took a step forward into the room. Something crunched beneath my shoe. Looking down, I discovered wooden debris littering the floor. It took me a few minutes to realize that what I saw must've been more wine racks at one point.

Someone had put a hole in the center of the wall. Presumably Geoff, still searching for the treasure, but now he knew where to find it. He must've found the journal after I left it on the nightstand. Another reason to kill Deborah and get her out of the way—what if she'd figured out the truth? That made more sense than her committing suicide.

To my surprise, on the other side of the hole, something glittered at me. All this time, Liam hadn't been lying. There was treasure inside the house!

One thing at a time. If there was stolen property here, Miriam and Deborah's murderer didn't get to be the one to claim it. It needed to be returned to its rightful owners.

Moving deeper into the room, I went to the hole to examine the booty. The opening in the wall was about six feet wide, maybe a couple of feet deep. Really more of a treasure cache or a hidden safe than anything else, although it was tall. It didn't take much away from the size of the wine cellar. A person would have to be really familiar with the house to know it was here.

Footsteps sounded behind me. I whirled around, heart pounding. Someone was in the house! A blur of motion whizzed by. I ducked. Air whooshed over my head, letting me know that I'd just missed getting hit by centimeters. Promptly forgetting all my training from Maria, I swung my arms wildly. Whoever it was jumped out of the way. I straightened up, prepared to face my attacker head-on.

Something hit me in the chest. I toppled backward, into the hole. My head banged against the far wall, making me see stars. I flailed wildly for balance. Before I could recover, someone grabbed my legs and flipped them upward. My phone dropped out of my pocket, clattering to the ground. My butt hit the ground, leaving me completely inside Liam's little storage room.

Space was tight in here. I could barely move, could barely gasp for breath, and I had no idea what Geoff—it had to be Geoff out there—would do if I came at him. He had the upper hand, not being stuck. All I'd have was the element of surprise. I figured I'd have one chance to lunge at him, knee him in the groin, throw myself out of the hole, and get past him up the stairs.

The odds weren't good, but I didn't have anything else to hold on to. If I stopped to do the math, I'd panic.

"Oh, Aly. What a pickle you've gotten yourself into." The voice was familiar, although muffled by the wall and possibly my fuzzy-headedness. "How are you going to get out of this one?"

I didn't answer, focusing instead of finding all my limbs and remembering how to breathe. As quietly as I could, I pulled myself upright, preparing to launch myself at Geoff's face before he could hit me with one of the shelves that used to line this wall.

Play dumb, I told myself.

"Sorry, Geoff, I seem to have tripped," I said. "Can you help me?"

A high-pitched giggle was my only response. So much for that. Finally, Geoff moved into view.

I fell backward against the wall. Because Geoff wasn't the one who attacked me. Through the carved opening in the stone wall, I found myself face-to-face with Deborah.

CHAPTER TWENTY-THREE

At the sight of a dead woman standing before me, I gaped for far too long. My mind whirled. In the past few months, I'd dealt with a lot of supernatural things. Psychics and visions and witches. I'd never dreamed I'd come face-to-face with a ghost.

Hold on. Ghosts didn't dig holes and search for treasure. They didn't push people. What did that make her—a zombie? What was going on here? How would Zombie Deborah get all the way to Miriam's house from the museum? Did she eat the brains of the police officers who found her?

Element one was hydrogen. Element two was helium. Element three was lithium, which I could use at the moment.

"Deborah?" My voice came out high, squeaky. As if I'd been sucking helium. More than a little panicked. "But you're dead! How are you here? What are you doing? Are you going to eat my brains?"

"Hello, Aly." Her smile didn't quite reach her eyes. "I

wish I could say it's lovely to see you again, but this is pretty darned inconvenient."

None of this made any sense. My brain spun as it tried to make sense of all the different things I knew. Deborah was Miriam's heir. Deborah was dead. Geoff was Deborah's heir.

Zombies didn't speak in complete sentences.

Ghosts weren't corporeal.

Unless she'd been turned into a vampire, Deborah was alive.

Miriam refused to marry Barry, which meant her will wouldn't automatically change. But she'd been about to sell the house. Deborah wanted the house. Geoff wanted the house. Deborah was dead. Deborah stood in front of me. The house had treasure. Deborah wanted the treasure. And she didn't want me to stop her from getting it.

For half a second, I allowed myself to wonder if the person in front of me was really Geoff and not Deborah. But why put on a costume to do excavation work in an empty basement? Besides, this person had Deborah's figure, and I just didn't see Geoff padding a bra to pretend to be his dead sister while searching an empty house for treasure. The dark circles under Deborah's eyes also suggested she wasn't wearing a ton of makeup.

Not knowing what else to say, I forced myself to let out an excited cry. Maybe if she thought I believed her, she'd start talking and tell me what I needed to know to go to the cops. "Thank goodness you're alive! Sam and I went to see you at the museum, and they said you were dead. I'm so glad they saved you!"

"Nice try," Deborah said dryly. "I know you've been investigating me, and I know you're not happy to see me alive."

"I wouldn't say I want you dead. But I'm confused, because I definitely saw your dead body on Sunday."

"No, you found *a* body," she said. "Once TSA stopped me from boarding my plane to Thailand, I knew something was up. Then I saw you and Sam waiting outside my apartment. I put on a wig and a pair of glasses and headed out."

A wig? The man in the car. "That was you! We thought it was Geoff."

"Who thought having a brother who makes horror movies would ever come in handy?" Lower, almost to herself, she said, "To be honest, I'd long since resigned myself to the idea of Geoff being completely useless."

Time to empathize, make her want to confide in me. "Brothers can be such a pain, can't they?"

"Mine is. Anyway, I set everything up at the museum after I saw you there Saturday night. I knew you weren't there for the exhibit."

"Sam was. He loves math."

She waved one hand. "He wasn't enough of a cover. Your conversation was too..."

"On point?"

"I wouldn't sound so smug if I were you. You're not leaving this room," she said.

Since Deborah blocked my only exit path, I didn't argue with her. I didn't know how fast she could move. Instead, I pressed the wall behind me, checking to see how sturdy it was. When Liam built this place, he had to include some way to access it, right? I needed to find a crack, a door, a button, anything. Preferably opening onto the other side and safety.

Meanwhile, I had to keep her talking. "Tell me how you did it. You set up the dummy. Then what? Sam and I talked to the police."

"Actor friends. I hired them."

This woman had somehow thought of everything. "You knew we'd get into your office?"

"Oh, yes. Changing my password to Aunt Miriam's birthday was a nice touch, don't you think? I figured you'd guess it easily enough."

I wanted to kick myself. If only the police officers hadn't caught me before I managed to examine "Deborah's" body. Surely one of us would have managed to figure out the truth if we'd gotten closer to Bessie. We may not be doctors, but we could probably tell the difference between a dead body and a prop once we started looking for a pulse.

"But why would you do it?" I asked. "You were already set to inherit everything."

"Inherit what?" She swept her arm around the room. "This was all that was left! Just the house, mortgaged to the hilt. Uncle Liam spent everything, lost it all in one business scheme after another. Geoff was like him in that way. It's why they got along so well."

"Are you sure?" I racked my brain but couldn't think what else to say. "Gloria seemed to think—"

She laughed hollowly. The humorless sound bounced off the walls, sending a chill down my spine. "Oh, Miriam did a good job keeping up appearances. But I knew. I was here every week, I helped her go through her bills. She had nothing left."

"There was a life insurance policy," I said. "You were the beneficiary unless Miriam remarried. You knew Barry had proposed to her, didn't you?"

"She refused, but she was starting to reconsider. She told me that she wanted to marry him," Deborah said. "If she did, he'd get a million dollars from the life insurance when she died, plus the house. Obviously, I couldn't let that happen. Not when I'm up to my eyeballs in debt."

"I thought the museum paid you pretty well."

"Sure, it does. But I've been investing the past few years in a hedge fund run by one of Geoff's friends. Geoff's an idiot, but this guy talks a good game. Went to Wharton. They short sell stock, then wait for the price to drop and buy again. It's perfect. Until it wasn't. Something sent one of the stock prices through the roof. My buy date came up, and all of a sudden, I owed a ton. There was no way to pay, and Miriam refused to give me a loan. Said I brought this whole thing on myself."

"I'm sorry," I said. "That's terrible. What are you doing here, now, though? You were planning to leave the country until you got stopped. What changed your mind?"

"Geoff did, funnily enough."

"The two of you are in this together?"

She snorted. "Oh, heck no. Not when this is all his fault to start. But I caught him on Saturday, searching this place for treasure. He talked about it all the way back to the city after the estate sale ended. To be honest, I'd never paid any attention to Liam's rantings of Geoff's wild theories. But after TSA stopped me from leaving, I knew I couldn't stay at my place. What if police came to talk to me? I decided to camp out here for a few days until I came up with a new plan."

"But Barry said the treasure was a tall tale. What made you believe it was real?"

"Once I got here, I found all this stuff Geoff had hidden in the basement. I knew immediately he'd been digging. I was so mad! But it wasn't until I realized he had Uncle Liam's diary that I realized there actually was treasure buried in this house. It's a heck of a lot more money than the life insurance policy, too. It's also untraceable," she said. "I drive over the Canadian border, I get a new identity, I vanish. It's perfect. Or it was, until you came along. Now I'm stuck with one more loose end to tie up."

"You could let me go," I said. "I won't tell anyone about any of this."

"Do I look like I was born yesterday?" she asked. "Now, it would be tough to make it look like you killed yourself or had a heart attack, but you could just... disappear! That's pretty easy. You're already here, in this unfortunate predicament. It'll be a pain to have to close the hole up, wait for you to die, and come back to reclaim my treasure, though. I'll have to come up with a better way."

A chill went down my spine. The look in her eyes told me that the semi-rational, seemingly reasonable Deborah I'd met at the estate sale was gone. This woman was on the verge of stealing a fortune, and she'd do anything to prevent me from getting in her way.

Element thirty-three was arsenic. Element thirty-four was selenium. I always liked that one. Selenium. Seemed peaceful. Element thirty-five was bromine.

Since Deborah was mostly talking to herself, there didn't seem to be a point in answering. I resumed my search of the tiny space, looking for the secret exit that would absolutely be there if this were a *Lifetime* Original Movie.

My little prison ran along the entire width of the wine cellar, from what I could tell, but was only a few feet deep. There had to be some other entry point, unless Liam's plan had been to hide the jewels and never return for them or knock the cellar down when he wanted some money. I pushed and prodded, poking my fingers into the mortar between the bricks. Other than me, the only thing in this cell was a stack of boxes, which someone (presumably Deborah) had already opened. Jewels spilled out of the top box: earrings and bracelets and some large, uncut gems. Diamonds could cut stone, right? I wonder if I could find the right one to help me dig my way out. Hypothetically, I might manage to carve a hole in the mortar and push through this wall before I ran out of air.

Yet I didn't see Deborah standing there and watching me dig my escape route, so my plan had some flaws unless she sealed me in. Which had the bigger, more immediate problem of reducing my air and taking my light.

Where was my phone? My hands went to my pockets, which should have held my phone and my keys. I hadn't thought about either of them since tumbling over the wall. My keys were still there, but my phone must have fallen out. There was one other thing, though: Barry's lighter.

As far as weapons went, a set of keys and a lighter weren't high on my list of "Things I'd Want to Defend Myself." But at the moment, it was all I had to work with, other than a pile of gemstones. Could I throw one at Deborah's head?

Sure, if I wanted to create a cooling breeze for her as it whizzed harmlessly by.

On the other side of the wall, Deborah ignored me entirely while she opened and closed drawers on the island. From the random mumblings reaching my ear, she either wanted something to tie me up with or something to knock me out. I didn't intend to stick around for her to find them. But then I saw the bottle of vodka and something clicked.

I hadn't had a drink since my twenty-first birthday, because that was the day my psychic powers materialized. Olive suggested that alcohol might affect my powers, and I'd never wanted to find out how. One day, Rusty and I planned to do some controlled experiments. But now...That was good vodka. Very high proof.

Putting my hand in my pocket, I rubbed my fingers over the lighter's cool surface. It was soothing. Then, summoning my courage, I cleared my throat. "Since you're going to kill me, how about one last request?"

"Do I look like I was born yesterday? You think I'm going to help you out or give your cell phone back so you can call for help?"

I shook my head. "Actually, I was thinking that my final hours might go a little better with some liquid courage. Could I have a shot of vodka?"

"You want the three-hundred-dollar bottle I bought to celebrate finding Liam's treasure?" She looked from the bottle on the island to me and back, then shrugged. "Whatever. It'll be the last thing you ever taste. You can use my glass. It's not like I'm going to give you the plague."

So much for hitting her with the bottle. Ah, well. As she opened the bottle and poured a scant inch of vodka into a glass, I used her movements to cover the sound of opening the top of the lighter. She brought me the glass, holding it out from several inches away, as if she thought I was going to grab her hand and somehow drag her into this space with me.

A brilliant idea, actually, but I had no idea how to pull it off. Besides, I had a different idea.

"Thank you." As I spoke, I thumbed the wheel on the lighter, grateful when a tiny flame flickered in the corner of my vision.

"You're welcome," she said. "You know, I kind of liked you. I'm sorry I have to kill you."

"I understand," I said. "Cheers!"

Lifting the glass, I tilted my head back, taking every possible drop into my mouth. Then I brought the lighter up, flame already lit, and spit the alcohol directly into Deborah's face.

She screamed. She dropped to the ground.

CHAPTER TWENTY-FOUR

When Deborah went down, I threw the glass at her. It probably wouldn't hurt her much, but I couldn't climb out holding it. Then I scrambled over the wall, hardly daring to look at Deborah. Only one thing was on my mind: escape. Pausing only to snatch my phone from the ground where it had fallen, I raced for the stairs. A scream of rage behind me told me that she wouldn't be down for long.

When I got to the top of the stairs, I thrust the door open. Footsteps pounded toward me. I stumbled through the door as Deborah wailed. "Aly! Help me!"

Nope, not born yesterday. Police could get her all the help they needed when they arrived. I slammed the door, threw the latch across it, and leaned back against the wood, gasping for breath. One of these days, I really did need to join a gym. I was lucky to be alive.

Deborah's fists pounding on the inside of the door reminded me that I wasn't home free yet. If she broke it down, she'd come after me. The back door was closer, but my car was out front. I raced for the foyer.

Outside, police sirens wailed. Had Deborah called from

the basement? That didn't make any sense. Two police cars screeched to a halt in front of me. I raised my hands as an officer exited each car.

"Deborah's trapped in the basement," I told the first one. "She killed Miriam and was trying to kill me."

Now that I was safe, my knees gave out. I sank to the grass, still gasping for air. A second later, a paramedic came to wrap a blanket over my shoulders. I waved away any other help.

Barry's car pulled to a stop in front of me. I staggered to my feet to greet him as police were bringing Deborah out of the house. She was screaming and fighting them, but when she saw Barry, she stopped.

"How could you?" Barry asked. "After Liam died, Miriam loved you more than anything in the world."

"Whatever," Deborah spat. "She said she loved me too much to help me buy my way out of debts. I'm in big trouble, and it's all her fault."

"It's not her fault you bought into your brother's scams," Barry said. "And it doesn't matter anymore. It's over."

Three police officers stepped up behind Barry. The one in front, a woman with red hair pulled into a French braid, stepped forward. "Deborah Peabody, you're under arrest for the murder of Miriam Peabody."

"What are you talking about?" She pointed at me. "That girl tried to kill me."

"We'll have plenty of time to sort that out down at the station. It'll be much easier for everyone if you cooperate."

"I'm innocent! I didn't do anything!" she yelled as the two officers who hadn't spoken pulled her hands behind her back and slapped handcuffs on her.

"She's lying," I said. "She confessed. She had access to

cyanide at work, and she was afraid Miriam would remarry, disinheriting her."

At that, Deborah's face turned purple. She lunged for me, nearly evading the officer's grasp. It took several minutes for them to subdue her while I cowered in place.

Finally, one of the officers explained her right to remain silent while Deborah glared at me furiously.

"Okay, fine, I did it. I would have gotten away with it, too, if it weren't for your meddling," she said. "Everyone was so sure Aunt Miriam died of natural causes. No one dreamed she'd been poisoned. They didn't even check! But no, you wouldn't let it go."

"I couldn't let it go," I said. "Miriam needed my help."

She was still ranting and raving when police hauled her away.

Barry stared at me for a long moment, hands in his pockets. "You did a very foolish thing just then, coming here by yourself."

"I know. I thought the place was deserted." At the thought of what might have happened, an overwhelming wave of gratitude hit me. "What are you doing here, anyway?"

"Olive called me, like you were supposed to."

"I suppose you called the police?"

"Only when I called and you didn't answer."

That must've been when my phone was on the floor of the wine cellar. I hadn't noticed. "Thanks."

"You're not welcome," he said. "Don't get me wrong. I'm glad Miriam will get justice. But next time? Wait for backup."

"Between you and me, I hope there isn't a next time. I've had enough of close calls for a long, long time." That reminded me. I brought his lighter out of my pocket. "This is yours, by the way. It saved my life."

"And they say smoking will kill you." He paused. "I've got something for you, too."

To my surprise, he reached into his wallet and pulled out a check. My eyes widened at all the zeros. "I can't accept this!"

"Yes, you can," he said. "When I called Olive last week, I told her I suspected foul play, and I would pay if you could prove it."

"This is—"

"—Exactly what you deserve. Take a lesson from an old man: know your worth. And you, Aly, are worth your weight in gold. I only wish I could give you more."

"But how? The estate was broke, right? That's what Deborah said."

"Was the estate broke? Or was that what Miriam wanted her money-grubbing relatives to think?"

A smile crossed my face. The more I knew about Miriam, the more I liked her. "I don't know what to say."

"Say, 'thank you, Barry.'"

"Thank you, Barry. Truly." The money in my hands would comfortably pay off my car and my school without needing more student loans. It might even cover graduate school for a year or two, if I stayed with Kevin. It was by far the most generous gift anyone had ever given me. "I'm sorry about Miriam. I know you loved her. Sorry for a minute I thought you might have killed her."

"I understand. Lying about our relationship probably didn't make me seem trustworthy." He wiped his eyes. "But I really did love her. That's one reason it was so important to find the truth. Now I can move on."

EPILOGUE

It took forever for Kevin to cut through the legal red tape needed for us to get back inside Destiny's Haven. I'd offered to put on my "Amy" costume and head back in with Tiffaneigh as her assistant. To say my brother wasn't amused would be putting it mildly.

So, I waited patiently, focusing on work and Kyle. In my spare time, I tried to track down Mallory to ask her about the skiing accident, but every lead turned into a dead end.

Sam and I managed three whole dinner dates where no one got murdered. I liked him more every day. We texted constantly. Even though it was early, I felt very optimistic about his upcoming graduation and return to Shady Grove at the end of the next school year.

In July, I helped Julie prepare her booth at the Shady Grove Scavenger Hunt. Turned out, my knowledge of chemistry helped her create some interesting new concoctions (and some terrible ones). Rusty and I teamed up to participate in the Scavenger Hunt, and we had a great time —but that was a story for another day.

When Kevin finally told me he'd gotten the necessary

paperwork, I was texting Olive to tell her I needed to leave work before he'd finished letting me know when he'd pick me up. By the time we pulled into the parking lot of Destiny's Haven, I was practically giddy with excitement. Today was the day: I could feel it!

"We're here to visit Mary Towne." Kevin placed his bar card and a sheet of paper on the desk. As Harmony looked up at him, he said, "I've got the conservatorship papers here. The facility can't keep her locked away as a prisoner."

"You're right, Mr. Reynolds, we can't," Harmony said.

"Great! Take me to her."

"I'd love to, but Ms. Towne checked out yesterday."

All of my happiness crashed down around me. No! She couldn't be gone. Kevin and I needed to get in, to have a real talk with her, to find out once and for all what happened to Katrina. Priscilla was supposed to help us find her. Once again, we were so close and everything was slipping away.

Before I could voice my dismay, Kevin intervened, addressing Harmony. "That's impossible. She was involuntarily committed."

"Yes, she was, by her doctor."

"I need to know who checked her out then."

"You do, do you?" Completely unfazed by his "lawyer tone," Harmony picked up the papers Kevin had left on the counter, slowly put on her reading glasses, and began to scan them. My brother waited patiently while I forced myself not to tap my foot on the floor or start texting Sam to complain about the delay. "You two are welcome to take a seat. This could be a while."

"No, thank you," Kevin said. "We'll stand."

While we waited, I pulled Kevin back and whispered. "Why wouldn't she call me before leaving? I gave her a cell phone last time I was here."

Loudly, Harmony said, "Patients are not permitted to have cell phones. Any contraband would have been confiscated."

My cheeks grew warm. "I mean...I'm sure she didn't have a phone. Where would she get it? How? Does she still have it?"

"Anything confiscated or left behind would be kept in a box for thirty days in case she returned."

"I'll take it," Kevin said. "As her authorized representative, I'm also entitled to collect all of Ms. Towne's belongings on her behalf."

"Mm-hmm," Harmony said. "Desperate for an old scrunchie and burner phone?"

Startled, I met her gaze. She wasn't impressed with me. They'd probably found the forbidden device shortly after I gave it to Priscilla, which might explain why I'd never heard from her.

When I didn't say anything more, Harmony pushed her glasses back up onto the bridge of her nose and turned back to the computer. After what felt like an eternity, she handed the paperwork back to Kevin. Then she picked up his bar card and examined it thoroughly. I half expected her to hold it up to the light like it might have a secret code written on it in milk. Finally, she turned to her computer. She tapped away on her keyboard for a few minutes before addressing us again. "Okay, thank you for your patience. Yes, I can tell you what happened. Ms. Towne's doctor arrived a couple of weeks ago with new paperwork insisting that she be transferred to another facility. Said she needed to be closer to family."

"We're her family!" I blurted out.

Harmony peered at me over the top of her glasses.

"Weren't you the one who caused her to have a breakdown last time you were here?"

"That wasn't my fault," I said. "Someone attacked us."

"She checked out weeks ago?" Kevin asked. "No one notified us."

"Yeah, it says right here." She named the date, and my eyes widened. That had been the day of the Shady Grove Treasure Hunt. Also a day where Kyle and I were out and about, not home at all. Using magic. Could it be a coincidence? Or had only the fact that we'd been in public all day saved him from danger?

Kevin glanced at me, letting me know he also caught the significance of the date, before turning back to Harmony. "Do you have the doctor's contact information? I'd like to speak with them. By removing Ms. Towne without the court's authority, they may be in contempt of the judge's order."

She muttered something under her breath about "lawyers" before meeting Kevin's eyes again. "Hold on, I'll print what we have. I don't want to get anyone in trouble with the judge. Here it is."

A printer on the desk beside her hummed to life, and we watched it spit out a page. I had to resist the urge to lean over the counter and snatch it up.

"Thank you so much for your help." Kevin gave Harmony a wide smile. She flushed, and I realized with a start that they were approximately the same age. Was my brother flirting? He was actually pretty charming when he wasn't brooding or watching baseball.

"I'm happy to help, Mr. Reynolds," she said. "Between you and me, there was something off about that doctor. I didn't trust her. But my supervisor said we had to let Ms. Towne go. We didn't know about the court order. I'm so sorry. There's nothing we can do now that she's checked out."

"It's okay," Kevin said. "You're not in any trouble. You're just doing your job."

She collected the papers from the printer and skimmed them before holding them out to me. "Here you go. Mary Towne left the facility on July 31. Checked out by Dr. Priscilla Huntington."

Did you enjoy *Sight Seering*? Then you'll love Seer Today, Gone Tomorrow

Just when Aly finally identified her sister-in-law's killer, they got away—and they're not alone.

Aly's on the case, but leads are few and far between. Meanwhile, another mystery arises: what do you get a psychic toddler for his fourth birthday? Aly wants to make her nephew's day, but the quest for the perfect gift skids to a halt when she finds the pet store trashed, a trail of blood, and the owner missing.

To make matters worse, someone powerful has cursed the residents of Shady Grove. Aly's powers vanish. Without her psychic gifts, how will Aly find Katrina's killer and save the pet store?

Seer Today, Gone Tomorrow

Preorder now from your favorite retailer

BY ADA BELL

<u>Shady Grove Psychic Mysteries</u>

Mystic Pieces
The Scry's the Limit
Sight Seering
Mystic Heirs: A Shady Grove Novella
Seer Today, Gone Tomorrow

ACKNOWLEDGMENTS

This book would never have happened without the expertise of Kristi LaMonica, who I cannot possibly thank enough for explaining how to distill DNA. I did name a museum after you, though, so I hope that's a good start. Any mistakes are mine alone. Thank you also to Stephany Wilson for answering my random questions about Long Island.

Thanks to Crystal, Marty, Wendy, and Tara for your feedback and editing. Thanks to Audrey for saving my butt. Thanks again to Victoria Cooper at La Viosin for knocking the cover out of the park.

I hope you enjoyed this book. If so, please consider leaving an honest review on Bookbub or with your favorite retailer.

ABOUT THE AUTHOR

Ada Bell is an award-winning and internationally best-selling author who thought that it would be cool to use a secret identity when writing mysteries. After all, who doesn't want a secret identity? She doesn't remember where the idea for the Shady Grove mysteries started, but she freely admits that Kyle is based on a certain precious toddler in her own life. Ada loves Scooby Doo, superhero movies, STEM heroines, and cake. Mmm, cake.

Find Ada online at www.adabell.com, or get access to sneak peeks, news and more by joining her Facebook group or mailing list. You can also follow her on Facebook or Twitter.

BOOKS WRITTEN AS LAURA
HEFFERNAN

The Reality Star Series
America's Next Reality Star
Sweet Reality
Reality Wedding

The Oceanic Dreams Series
Time of My Life

The Gamer Girls Series
She's Got Game
Against the Rules
Make Your Move

Push and Pole Series
Poll Dancer
The Accidental Senator

Finding Tranquility
Anna's Guide to Getting Even